Legacy of LOVE

Legacy of LOVE

ESSENCE BESTSELLING AUTHOR

DONNA HILL

ARABESQUE®

Recycling programs
for this product may
not exist in your area.

LEGACY OF LOVE

ISBN-13: 978-0-373-53455-5

Copyright © 2011 by Donna Hill

www.kimanipress.com

Printed in U.S.A.

This book is dedicated to all my loyal fans.
Thanks for your support.

Chapter 1

Zoe struggled to concentrate. But the harder she tried the more difficult it was to focus. She could almost feel his strong hands exploring her body. Her eyelids fluttered open as a soft, longing moan escaped her lips, reluctantly pulling her back to reality. She blinked rapidly and inhaled a shuddering breath, as she took in her surroundings amidst the storage room.

Back to work. Focus, she thought. Yet every day it was becoming more and more tiring. The fantasies were becoming almost lifelike, and the episodes of arousal were no longer confined to her dreams. The images appeared unexpectedly—behind her eyelids, stirring a tingling sensation as the fabric of her clothing brushed against her skin—any time of day or night. She breathed in slowly and deeply.

Zoe knotted her shoulder-length hair atop her head and continued to carefully unwrap the thick packaging that surrounded the five-foot tall wooden fertility statues. She'd been waiting weeks for them to be delivered, by the time they arrived from South Carolina earlier that morning. She peeled away the last layer of wrapping as the air momentarily caught in her throat. Her pulse was racing so fast, it was as if she was meeting a blind date for the first time.

Awestruck, she stepped back to get a better look. The rich ebony wood was polished to a smooth, shiny finish. The intricate hand-carved details captured every feature of the figures of the man and woman, from the sword and mango that he carried in his hands to the infant that she carried in hers. There seemed to be a warm glow radiating around them. But Zoe chalked it up to her overactive imagination or more likely the sun beaming down from the skylight overhead. The pair of sculptures was on loan from the Ripley Museum in South Carolina. And as head curator at the High Museum in Atlanta, it was her responsibility to search the globe for the best works of art for the museum's exhibits and collections. She was also responsible for ensuring their safe-keeping once the items were on display.

There were so many myths surrounding the beautifully carved totems—the most prominent being that touching the figures was an antidote to infertility. According to some of the stories, when the fertility sculptures were first put on display after having been purchased and brought to America from the Ivory Coast, within months, more than a dozen women who worked at the Ripley Museum became pregnant after touching the statues.

As with all urban legends, the story spread like wildfire and the fertility figures became the art world's equivalent of the miracle at Lourdes.

Zoe smiled. Although she came from a long line of conjure women and a family history filled with prophecies and curses, if she didn't believe the stories told by her Nana, her mother and her aunties, she certainly wasn't buying into the myth of the fertility totems. She didn't believe in all that mumbo jumbo, even if the dreams she'd been having were becoming more frequent and the hazy vision of a man was getting closer and his voice clearer, night after night.

Some mornings she'd awaken shaken and confused. She had an overwhelming feeling that if she had been able to hold on to sleep for a bit longer, the face that appeared in her dreams would materialize. It was ridiculous, of course. Yet, it was on days like today when she'd find herself scrutinizing everyone she passed on the street, secretly hoping to recognize him. She shook her head, dispelling the idea as mere silliness.

By nature she was a realist and her profession

demanded that she deal in facts and what was tangible. Sure, she was going to be thirty years old in three months, and she knew that upon her thirtieth birthday the legacy of women of the Beaumont clan would be upon her. But that didn't mean that she believed that she was the one who would break the curse that had plagued the Beaumont women for generations. Besides, if any part of the curse were true, she needed a man. And *that* she didn't have. She stared at the fertility couple.

A feeling of warmth began to build inside her, starting at her feet and slowly inching its way upward through her body. A thin line of perspiration formed at her hairline and her eyesight began to get cloudy. All of a sudden, the statues seemed to vibrate.

"Zoe, there you are."

Zoe jumped as if she'd been startled by an intruder. Her fingertips tingled and her heart raced as if she'd run a half marathon. She blinked several times to clear her vision, turned and forced herself to smile.

"Hey, Mike."

Mike Williams was one of the assistant curators. She'd brought him on once she'd settled into her position, and there wasn't a moment that she'd regretted her decision.

Mike was an expert in African art and antiquities dating back to the early 1800s. It was Mike who'd helped her negotiate the deal to get the fertility statues to the High Museum. And he wasn't bad to look at, either. The girls didn't call him "Big Mike" for no reason. With his smooth, Hershey chocolate-coated skin dripping over six-plus feet of sculpted muscle, Mike could have easily been bronzed and put on display.

"They're real beauties," he said, stepping up beside her.

"Hmm, yes, they are," she murmured gradually coming back down to earth. For an instant, she wondered if it was the image of Mike that haunted her dreams. *Ridiculous.*

"Do you buy into the whole fertility thing?" he asked, slowly walking around the statues, admiring the finely sculpted details.

Zoe sputtered a laugh. "You're kidding, right? You know me better than that. I believe in science and things that I can prove, not myths." No matter that her family believed otherwise.

"Just checking," he teased, rubbing the statue. "Why don't you give it a rub?"

She puckered her lips. "I will, just to prove you wrong." She ran her hand along the smooth ebony surface and a mild charge of electricity shot up her arm. She pulled her hand back. "Satisfied?" she said, a bit shaken as she spun away.

Mike's deep laughter followed her out of the storage room. Zoe got on the freight elevator, thankful to be alone. She got off the elevator on the second floor and walked along the corridor—flanked by cool, dove gray-colored walls—to her small office, and shut the door behind her.

What was going on? She did not feel like herself today, she thought, taking a seat behind her cluttered desk piled high with exhibit catalogues and research notes. She was sure it had something to do with the dreams she'd been having, which had become more vivid in the past few weeks—so much so that they were affecting her during her waking hours. Like today. What other explanation could there be for her reaction to the statues other than the lack of a good night's sleep?

She drew in a long calming breath. The opening of the exhibit unveiling the statues was in two weeks. She had plenty to do and no time to dwell on—well, whatever it was that was happening to her. Tonight she was determined to get some well-deserved rest and be prepared and clear-headed for the big event.

Zoe scoured through piles of research materials making notes on new finds and reading the latest news on African American museum collections across the country. She made some phone calls, and sent off a few emails. When she looked up at the clock above her door, she was stunned to see that it was past noontime. She pushed away from her desk, closed her eyes and stretched her arms high above her head. A whiff of a strongly male scent wafted toward her nose. Her eyes flew open, so sure she would find a man standing in her office. But she was completely alone.

Her gaze darted around the room, stopping in every corner. She gave a short shake of her head. Food, she needed food. She was operating on very little sleep and an empty stomach. She pulled open her bottom desk drawer and took out her purse.

Taking her suit jacket from the back of her chair she walked out of her office in search of food. Maybe she'd take a stroll over to her friend Sharlene's office and see if she was free for lunch.

"I'm going out for a while," she said to Mike, who was putting brochures out at the information desk. "I'll be back in about an hour."

"Enjoy."

"Thanks."

Zoe stepped out into the balmy spring afternoon. The sky was clear, and there was a crispness in the air. As usual, the streets of Atlanta were dotted with tourists and lunch-goers. She loved the city even as she missed her home and family in Louisiana.

Her mother, Mariya, had begged her to come home for a visit and she'd been putting it off with all that she had to do at work. But the urge to see her family was growing stronger every day. Maybe she could take a quick trip home for a weekend as soon as the exhibit opened, she thought as she turned down Peachtree Street in the direction of Sharlene's office. Mike could handle things in her absence.

She stopped in front of Moore Designs and opened the glass front door. The reception area of Moore Designs looked like a page from an interior design magazine. The walls were painted in bold colors, which complemented the sleek modern furnishings. Low couches and chairs provided a comfortable seating arrangement, set off by rugs that covered the hardwood floors. Eclectic wall art covered every inch of the space behind the reception desk.

For two years Sharlene had been the host of *Moore Designs* on HGTV. Although it gave her a high profile and droves of clients, the time she spent away from her design studio and from friends and family was more than she'd wanted to.

"Hi, Cynthia," Zoe said, greeting the front desk receptionist.

"Hi, how are you?"

"I'm good."

"How's everything coming with the opening?"

"Right on schedule. The statues arrived this morning, actually."

"They're getting a lot of buzz in the art world. Congrats on acquiring them."

"Thanks. It was definitely a team effort. Is Sharlene around?"

"Sharl is in her office. Go on back."

"Thanks."

Zoe walked down the hallway with its cool white

walls, and turned a corner to Sharlene's office. Her door was open.

"Hey, girl," she said, poking her head in.

Sharlene looked up from examining a batch of fabrics. Her sandy brown eyes lit up in her golden butter-tone face. She took off her glasses and set them on the desktop. "Hey. This is a surprise. I thought you'd have your hands full with the shipment today."

Zoe walked inside the office, which was definitely a reflection of Sharlene's personality and taste. The office was filled with design ideas that included vibrant fabric swatches, see-through drawers filled with marble, granite and wood samples, easels for her drawings, a drafting table, decorating accessories, colored pencils and paints. Zoe lifted a stack of magazines from a club chair and plopped down, suddenly feeling exhausted.

"You look like you could use a vacation," Sharlene said, noticing the sluggishness reflected in Zoe's tired-looking eyes. "Still not sleeping?"

Zoe shook her head and covered her mouth as she yawned. "I wish what I was doing was sleeping, but the dreams…"

Sharlene leaned back in her Herman Miller chair. "Still the same?"

"Yes, only more intense." Without warning her nipples hardened and the tiny bud between her thighs began to throb as images of the man who came to her in her dreams, the faceless man who made passionate love to her emerged in her mind. Her nostrils flared as her pulse quickened. She hadn't told Sharlene everything, not the parts about the faceless seducer who left her trembling with longing.

"Are you all right? You look flushed."

Zoe quickly shook her head. "Fine. Just tired."

Even Sharlene, who was as open-minded as they came, would think she was losing it if Zoe told her what had been going on at night. "And hungry." She forced a grin. "Can you get away for a bit?"

"Sure. My eyes were starting to cross looking at all these fabrics." She stood and took her purse from the shelf behind her desk. "Want to head over to Gladys Knight's place?"

"I was thinking the same thing. We should be able to get a table. It's still early."

The two friends walked out together staying on Peachtree Street to the restaurant three blocks away. The locale was famous not only because of its owner but for its mouth-watering menu, specifically the chicken and waffles, the house specialty. After a short wait, they were seated in a booth by the window and their orders were taken.

"You look like you could use a drink to go with that vacation," Sharlene commented, once the waitress was gone. "Is something else bothering you?" She gazed steadily at Zoe.

Zoe lowered her eyes then finally focused on Sharlene. "This is going to sound totally crazy."

"Maybe, but tell me anyway."

Zoe leaned back, stretched her arms out in front of her and cupped her water glass. "The dreams are more than…just dreams."

Sharlene's perfectly arched brows rose. "Okay, so what are they?"

"They're physical."

"Physical?"

"Yeah." She leaned closer. "He comes to me in my sleep," she said under her breath.

"What?" Sharlene said in confusion.

"The image of a man… He comes to me in my sleep, and…he makes love to me." She swallowed and realized how ridiculous it sounded.

Sharlene was quiet for a moment. "You dream about being made love to?"

"Yes."

"By a stranger?"

"Yes, but it's as if I know him." Her voice was beginning to take on a desperate edge. "But I can't see him. Not really." She shook her head. "Forget it. It doesn't make sense." She took a sip of her water.

"Zoe, remember what Nana Zora said," Sharlene reminded her gently.

Zoe's eyes jumped, as she stared at Sharlene, whose earnest expression seemed to invite a response. Sharlene was as much a family member as any blood relation, and had been privy to Zoe's Nana, her mother and aunts' tale of the Beaumont women's curse. Unlike Zoe, Sharlene was fascinated by it all, and wished that her own family history was as exotic and exciting.

"Well, come on. Your thirtieth birthday is in three months. Nana said—"

"Don't! Don't start. Okay." She rolled her eyes and looked away.

Sharlene leaned across the table. "What if it's true?" she said in a low whisper. "Wouldn't that be too fabulous and romantic?"

The waitress appeared with their lunch. When Zoe glanced up to thank her, she caught a glimpse in the corner of her eye of the broad back of a man who was walking out the front door. Blood rushed to her temples. She jumped, knocking over the glass of water on the table. In the moments of confusion and apologies, Zoe lost sight of him.

"What in the world is the matter with you?" Sharlene asked, checking around for any more puddles of water on the table.

"I…I thought I saw him." She shook her head. "I'm sorry. Exhaustion is getting the better of me."

Sharlene dabbed at the last bit of water. "You saw him?" she asked with a look of confusion.

Zoe waved her hand. "Forget it. Let's eat."

Sharlene studied the faraway look in Zoe's eyes and believed more than ever that the Beaumont legacy was real and her friend was simply unwilling to admit it.

Chapter 2

Jackson Treme continued on his walk back to his car with his bag of fried chicken and waffles, completely unaware of how his tall, lean figure cut a sharp outline against the busy downtown landscape, or how many admiring women's eyes took second looks as he passed. His thoughts were elsewhere.

He'd had the strangest sensation while he was waiting on his take-out order, a kind of energy that seemed to suddenly flow through his body. He felt strong, almost invincible. Inwardly he chuckled. How crazy was that? It was probably from inhaling the spicy aroma of the food that had his senses on high alert.

He stopped in front of his car. A soft, very

feminine scent wafted by him. He turned, looked left then right. Nothing. He released a long breath. These odd feelings that he'd been experiencing had begun a few weeks ago.

At first he thought it was simply the stress of moving from New Orleans to Atlanta, finding a house and taking on a new job. But he'd never been one to be thrown off balance by stress.

He opened the car door and got in, shut the door behind him and stuck the key in the ignition. Just as he looked up, in the distance, he spotted two women emerging from the restaurant. The car suddenly filled with the same heavenly scent. That feeling of power flowed through his body. He turned the key in the ignition, but his main focus was seeing *her* face. The car sputtered and shut off. *What the…* He turned the key again, gave it some gas. The engine whined and shut off. Without thinking, he hopped out of the car and jogged down the block. By the time he reached the corner they were nowhere in sight. His broad shoulders slumped. He stood on the corner like a lost tourist as passersby walked around him. Realizing how ridiculous he was behaving, he finally walked back to his car and slid behind the wheel. He turned the key and the car hummed to life.

"I've been thinking of taking a quick trip home," Zoe was saying as they walked into Pinkberry's frozen yogurt parlor.

Sharlene got in line behind Zoe. "Flying or driving?"

Zoe glanced over her shoulder. "Why?" she asked with a grin.

"You know I'm always up for a road trip."

Zoe twisted her lips in feigned contemplation. "Okay, road trip. Can you take Friday off?"

"Of course, my sister. That is the joy of owning your own business." She grinned broadly, exposing the teasing gap between her pearly white front teeth.

"If we leave by six we can be there by one."

"Sounds like a plan."

"How can I help you?" the young woman behind the counter asked.

"Two large mangos, to go," Zoe said and took out her Pinkberry purchase card to be stamped. The frozen yogurt place was Zoe and Sharlene's guilty pleasure. They'd bought enough frozen yogurt to own stock in the company.

"Why do we love this stuff so much?" Sharlene cooed as she took her first lick.

"I have no idea." Zoe swallowed the naturally sweet treat and sighed in delight.

They pushed through the doors and back out into the afternoon.

"I'm going to head back," Zoe said and kissed Sharlene's cheek.

"I need to make a stop first. Talk to you later."

They waved and headed off in opposite directions.

* * *

Zoe returned to the museum and was pleased to find that foot traffic had picked up in her absence. Museums were struggling all over the country and were usually the first institutions to feel the cuts in grants and sponsorship. Part of her role was to seek out funding; the funding that not only helped to pay staff but covered the costs of installing new works and putting up shows.

At times it was difficult. But the High Museum was more fortunate than most, and at least for now she could continue to look for those rare pieces that would attract crowds.

She crossed the expanse of the main exhibit floor, took the first right turn and walked down the empty corridor that echoed her footsteps to her office at the end of the hallway. If she was planning to take off on Friday, she needed to make sure that everything was in order. Even though Mike was more than capable of handling any problems in her absence, she'd rather not leave anything to chance. As she was settling down behind her desk, her body suddenly grew warm and a heady, manly scent drifted under her nose. Her heart thumped in her chest. She felt light-headed as if she'd stood up too quickly.

"Hey, how was lunch?"

Zoe blinked, gripped the armrests of her chair and forced herself to focus.

Mike stepped in. A frown drew a line between his brows. "You, okay? You looked frightened."

Zoe swallowed and ran her tongue across her dry lips. "Yeah, I'm fine." She made herself smile. "Frightened?" She sputtered a laugh and turned on her computer. "Of what, you?" she teased.

Mike checked her out for a moment more. "Yeah, okay." He shrugged. "I signed off on the schedule for next week and Linda has a problem with it. Linda always has a problem. If it's not the schedule, it's taking inventory or whatever it is she's supposed to be doing. If I say something to her to then I'm a bully. So maybe you want to talk to her. If it were up to me, she'd be pounding the pavement."

He leaned against the door frame, looking too enticing for words.

Zoe cleared her throat. She knew Linda's real motive. Linda had a thing for Mike and rather than be upfront about it, she used her energy to give him a hard time. Very junior high school as far as Zoe was concerned, but it wasn't her place to say anything to Mike about Linda. But her behavior was affecting her work, and that was a problem. "I'll have a talk with her before I leave. And speaking of leaving, I'm taking Friday off. I'm driving down to see my family."

"Cool. For how long?"

"Just the weekend. I'll be back on Monday. Sharlene is going with me."

Mike nodded. He pushed away from the door. "Please talk to your girl."

"I will. I promise."

"See you later." He turned and walked away.

Zoe folded her hands on top of her desk. *Could it be Mike?* she wondered. She shook her head. Now she was starting to think like her crazy family and her even crazier best friend. But as much as she tried, it was getting harder to ignore the feelings.

Jackson returned to his two-bedroom town house following his early evening run and went straight to the living room to turn on his 52-inch flat-screen television. It was his biggest purchase since moving into his new space. How many mornings had he awakened on the used leather couch, having fallen asleep in front of the flat screen?

There was a time falling asleep on the couch would have never happened. Instead of being eager to settle down in front of the television with a stack of papers to grade, he would look forward to undressing Carla and loving every inch of her body.

He pointed the remote at the television, kicked off his sneakers and stretched out on the couch. Carla was in his rearview mirror. It had been more than two years since they'd seen or spoken to each other. "It was him, not her," he'd said to the woman he'd thought he would marry. He'd tried to explain, to erase the look of hurt and disbelief from her eyes. The truth was he couldn't explain it to himself.

In the months leading up to their breakup, he'd felt himself pulling away from Carla as if drawn by some unseen force—the same force that brought him to Atlanta. The same force that filled his dreams at night, clouded his thoughts during the day and the scent that wafted under his nostrils when he least expected it. Like today.

He surfed through the channels and finally settled on MSNBC. He was still bummed by the changing lineup, but it was still one of the best cable news channels on the air. He crossed his feet at the ankles, but instead of concentrating on the latest developments in the Middle East, his thoughts segued to the strange feelings he'd experienced at the restaurant and the brief glimpse of that woman. He exhaled a deep breath. The woman he *thought* he had to see. He pressed his fingers over his eyes. Whatever was going on with him seemed to have escalated in the past few weeks. But in the midst of all the weirdness, he knew somehow this was where he was meant to be. For what, he wasn't sure. At some point it would all work itself out.

He was between dozing and half listening to Rachel Maddow when the vibrations of his cell phone broke into the lazy rhythm that was lulling him to sleep. Groaning, he turned to his side and dug his cell phone out of his sweatpants pocket. He held the iPhone up in front of him. His sister's name and number were lit up on the screen.

"Hey, sis."

"Did I wake you?"

"No. Just watching a little TV. Whatsup?" He stifled a yawn.

Michelle chuckled. "You were always such a bad liar. But since I woke you up, how are you?"

He tucked his hand behind his head. "Aw, now why do we have to start off with the name-calling?" he teased. His twin sister was more than a sibling. They were best friends. Jackson often felt bad that he didn't have that same level of connection with their older brother, Franklin. But Franklin was fifteen years older than his twin brother and sister and they were as much a surprise to him—upsetting his status as the only child—as their arrival was to their stunned parents. In their years growing up, Franklin was more of a father, rather than an older brother. Long before they were out of grade school, Franklin was off to college, and then marriage with children of his own.

"It's true," she volleyed back. "You can pretend with everyone except me. Those are the rules. Anyway, you've been on my mind all day. Is everything cool?"

Jackson stared up at the ceiling for a moment. Before he'd left New Orleans for Atlanta, he'd confessed to his sister about the strange pull he'd been feeling, and that somehow his destiny was in Atlanta.

"It's getting stronger," he finally said.

Michelle was quiet for a moment. "Anything new...different?"

"I thought I saw her today."

"What? Really? What did she look like?"

"Whoa, hold on." He chuckled. "I mean I didn't actually *see* her. I kind of thought I might have caught a glimpse of her." As soon as the words were out of his mouth he knew how ridiculous they sounded.

"Hmm, like an impression," Michelle deduced.

Jackson grinned. If anyone could understand it would be Michelle. "Exactly." He went on to explain what had transpired earlier in the day.

"You made the right decision, Jackson, about everything. Keep opening yourself and the answers will come. I firmly believe that."

"So do I, sis."

They talked for a while longer about the family, their respective jobs and then Michelle revealed the other reason for her call. "Carla is getting married. The announcement was in the *Time-Picayune* last weekend."

The news barely stirred him. He was only mildly surprised that he didn't feel something more. "I'm happy for her. I wasn't the one."

"I want you to be happy, too. And my sixth sense tells me that it's only a matter of time."

"I'm going to hold you to that."

"You do that. I haven't been wrong yet. Listen, gotta run. We'll talk soon. Okay?"

"Yep. Tell Travis hello and give my niece a kiss for me."

"Will do. Love ya."

"Back at you."

Jackson placed the phone on the coffee table. Michelle was right. Her intuition was always on point. How it was going to finally play out, however, was anyone's guess.

Chapter 3

Zoe decided to forego the ten-minute drive to work and opted to walk instead, making up for her missed visits to the gym over the past week. She strolled, her mind and spirit lifted by the warmth of the morning sun and the soft breeze that carried the scent of blooming flowers and the secret aroma of the South—rich, lush, troubled, ever changing… and something burning. She quickened her pace.

The sound of screaming sirens drew closer and when she reached the corner she saw grey smoke billowing out of one of the buildings on the street. A crowd began to gather even as the fireman urged them back.

Zoe's hand flew to the center of her chest. "Oh,

no." Slowly she approached the growing crowd. The hair on her arms and at the back of her neck seemed to rise. Her heart pounded. For a moment she felt light-headed and swayed where she stood. The scene in front of her started to recede.

"Are you all right?"

A strong arm gripped her around the waist, keeping her from sinking to her knees. Her rescuer guided her across the street and helped her to sit down on a bench.

Zoe sucked in long breaths of air trying to clear her head.

"Smoke must have gotten to you," the voice was saying.

She shook her head to clear it and looked into the most incredible pair of dark eyes that were staring at her with concern. She knew those eyes, that voice. But that was not possible. She didn't know this man. Fear crept through her body. She wanted to run, but she couldn't make her body move.

"Sit right here, I'm going to get you some water."

She watched him rise and tower above her, the same image that came to her in her dreams. Her stomach dipped and rose and dipped again. She gripped the arm of the bench.

He hurried down the crowded street, weaving his way around the clutch of bodies, trucks and fire hoses.

Another fire truck screamed onto the street. Flames leaped from one building to the next. Shouts rang out from the crowd as they were urged back by fireman and now the police. News vans pulled onto the street.

Zoe got to her feet and was suddenly caught up in the crowd that was being pushed back by the police.

"Move it back! Move it back!"

Zoe merged with the throng, swept along with the wave of bodies until she was ushered off of the street. The farther she moved from the scene the clearer her thoughts became. She tried to spot him, convince herself that he was real and not some trick of her imagination. He was gone, as if he never existed. He probably didn't, she told herself as she took an alternate route to the museum.

By the time she arrived she felt exhausted, drained as if she hadn't slept and then worked all day. Yet, it was barely nine o'clock, and for the first time in weeks she'd actually slept through the night.

Zoe greeted the security guard, swiped her ID card through the slot and proceeded to her office. Once inside she slipped out of her suit jacket and just as she was about to hang it up on the hook, that familiar scent filled her senses. She pulled the jacket to her nose. Instead of hints of smoke and soot from the fire it smelled like…*him.*

Her hands shook and the jacket fell from her fingers.

The phone on her desk rang and she jumped a half inch off the floor.

Exhaling deeply, she returned to her desk and picked up the phone. "Zoe Beaumont." Slowly she lowered herself into her seat.

"Zoe, it's Mama."

Zoe sat straight up. Her mother never called her at work. They saved their long, often giggly conversations for Sunday afternoons.

"Mama, what is it?"

"Your grandmother's been asking for you."

"Is Nana all right? What's wrong?"

"I…I don't know. She's getting more distant everyday. Most days she thinks it's fifty years ago. The only thing that makes sense is her asking for you. You have to come, baby."

"I was planning to come this weekend. But if you think I need to leave earlier I will. Sharlene is driving down with me." She could feel her mother's relief seep through the phone.

"Good. I'll fix up the guest room. Thank you, baby."

"Ma, you don't have to thank me. Please. You take it easy. Where are Aunt Flo and Aunt Fern?"

"Taking turns looking after your grandmother. She hardly notices…" Her voice cracked. "Just come as soon as you can."

"I will. I promise. Give my love to Nana."

Zoe replaced the phone in the cradle. She'd heard the anxiety and fear in her mother's voice. Miraya Beaumont was as reliable as the North Star. Nothing threw her off course. So to hear uncertainty in her mother's voice completely unnerved Zoe.

She swiveled her chair toward her computer, and powered it up, intent on finding a flight out of Atlanta that wouldn't bankrupt her. Just as the search engine got her to the website, Mike came in.

"Hey. Good morning. What's up?"

"Morning. Did you hear about the big fire up on 9th?"

"I was there."

Mike frowned. "What?"

"I mean, I decided to walk today and literally walked right into it. Awful." She shook her head at the memory. "It looked like the whole block was going to go up in flames." A little shiver went through her as the image of the man of her dreams invaded her senses.

"It's been on all the news channels, but it looks like they finally got it under control."

"Thank goodness. I hope no one got hurt."

"Yeah." He came around to the side of her desk. "Here are the bills for last month's shipments."

"Just leave them. I'll take care of it." The Delta Air Lines home page filled her computer screen.

Mike dropped the folders on her desk and spied the page. "Vacation?"

"Not really. I need to get home in a hurry."

"Everything cool?"

"It's my grandmother." She keyed in her information. "I was planning on driving down this weekend, but my mom called just a little while ago and she sounded…" Her fingers flew across the keys. She sniffed, pulled open her desk drawer to get her purse. She took out her wallet and flipped through the compartments for her Visa card, keyed in the numbers and waited.

"I think it's best that I don't wait." She swallowed the knot in her throat.

"Hey, do what you have to do. Family first. I got this. Don't worry about it."

Zoe forced a smile. "Thanks."

The screen flashed her confirmation number and the button to print her itinerary and boarding pass. She pressed *Print*.

Mike placed a large comforting hand on her shoulder. She tilted her head toward him and blinked back the tears burning in her eyes.

"Need a lift to the airport?"

"No. My flight is at 6:00 a.m. I wouldn't do that to anyone," she said, only half joking.

"It's not a problem." He stepped back. "Just let me know."

She bobbed her head. "Thanks."

Mike strolled out.

Mike really was a great guy. He was intelligent, hard working, fun, sexy. He definitely had it all. She sighed. But even with all that she couldn't take her mind off of what had happened to her less than an hour earlier. The impression of him, his scent, the look in his eyes, the arch of his cheekbones, the curve of his bottom lip.

Her heart raced as the image of her night stalker come to life replayed in her mind. Yet her pulse didn't race with fear or trepidation, but rather with anticipation and curiosity. Who was he really and why did he have that kind of effect on her? Was he really the man of her dreams? She logged off of the Delta site and laughed lightly to herself. *There you go being ridiculous.* If that were true, then it meant that she really was buying into all that foolishness that her mother, aunts and grandmother had been saying for as long as she could remember. *Ridiculous.*

Her grandmother. Nana Zora was the thread that held the fabric of her family together. She couldn't imagine her family without Nana Zora. Growing up, Nana had been more of a mother to her than her own mother, Miraya, had ever been. Her mother was an aspiring singer and spent most of Zoe's youth and young adulthood traveling the country, moving from one nightclub or lounge to the other. One disappointment too many and a cigarette short of losing her voice altogether, Miraya returned to her hometown of New Orleans and tried to put her life back together and bond with a daughter she barely knew.

It was Nana Zora who encouraged Zoe to pursue her love of the arts, which she insisted Zoe had inherited from her mother. Zoe believed differently.

It was her Nana who nurtured her passion for art and painting and her interest in history and other cultures. By the time Miraya Beaumont returned to New Orleans, Zoe had traveled and studied and mapped out her future—without the help or guidance of her mother. It took time and a lot of patience, forgiveness and a lot of coaxing from Nana but they'd finally found their way to each other.

It was also her grandmother who firmly believed in the legacy of the Beaumont women. As much as she didn't want to buy into the old wives' tale and family lore, everything that her grandmother, her mother and her aunts had said was slowly coming to pass.

She picked up the phone to call Sharlene and let her know about her change of plans and wondered what her grandmother would say about the inexplicable events that had made their way into her life.

"Tomorrow morning?"

"I don't want to wait until the weekend. My mother sounded scared and she never sounds scared."

"Let me rearranged my schedule. Give me your flight number and I'll book my ticket as well."

"Sharl, that's too much. You don't have to—"

"I know that. I want to. She's my Nana, too. And you're my sister. I'll call you back in a few."

Zoe squeezed the receiver in her hand and briefly

shut her eyes. She wouldn't admit to Sharlene just how much she needed her. She didn't have to. Sharlene already knew.

Chapter 4

Jackson shut the door of his Explorer and walked across the parking lot of Clark-Atlanta University. The acrid scent of smoke still lingered in his nostrils and the image of the woman in his mind. When he'd literally stumbled upon her he couldn't believe it at first. He was certain she was the same woman he'd spotted the other day. He could kick himself for leaving her even for a second before he found out who she was.

He cut across the lot and entered the campus grounds, followed the path to the humanities building and tugged open the ornate wood door.

"Mornin' Professor Treme," said a young man in a freshly pressed white shirt with an armload of books.

"Have a productive day, Mahlik," Jackson offered before turning the corner toward his office. His first class wasn't for another twenty minutes.

"Hey, Jackson!"

Jackson glanced over his shoulder. It was his colleague Levi Fortune hurrying toward him.

"I wanted to talk with you about something," he said, coming to a stop alongside Jackson.

"Levi, if it's about taking over one of your classes again, the answer is no." He stuck the key into the lock of his office door.

"Aw, come on man. Just one more time. I've got to put the finishing touches on my dissertation. I have to defend it in three weeks."

"You should have taken a sabbatical." Jackson shook his head in a combination of dismay and annoyance. He could only imagine the stress that Levi was under trying to teach three classes and get his second doctorate degree. The man was no dummy, but he was going to kill himself in the process. Jackson turned to him and grinned.

"Okay. You know I will." He pushed open the office door. "Take a load off." Jackson walked in and dropped his soft brown leather satchel on top of his desk then walked around his desk to open the window blinds.

Levi dropped down into the lone chair in the tight space and stretched out his long legs. "You know I owe you."

"Big time. I'll think of something. So how's the work coming?"

Levi linked his fingers together. "Man, if I survive this, I'm done. For real." He chuckled lightly. "I don't remember it being this hard."

"Ancient languages are no joke, man." He lowered himself into his squeaky leather chair. "So, when you get your degree I have to call you Dr. Dr. Fortune or what?"

"You can just call me doctor. The rest of them can call me Double D."

They broke out laughing and exchanged a pound.

"What's your day looking like?"

"Not too bad. I have one class this morning and one right after lunch," Jackson said. "How about you?"

"Two before lunch. Department meeting this afternoon and then I'm done. Wanna grab a beer or something later?"

"Yeah, yeah sure. Meet you around five?"

"Cool." He got up from the chair. "And thanks again for standing in for me."

"We gotta help each other out."

"So I'll see you around five. Over at Smitty's?" Levi said on his way out.

"Yeah. I'll be there and the beers are on you."

"No doubt. Later, man."

Jackson unsnapped his satchel and took out a folder stuffed with graded papers, notes and the lesson plan for his upcoming class. He checked his watch. He had about ten minutes. He leaned back in his seat and went over his notes, making sure that he had plenty of material to cover during the ninety-minute session. Some days his class arrived fully prepared and were totally engaged. Other times, it was like talking to comatose patients. He hoped today wasn't one of those days. He wasn't up for it. It was taking all of his concentration to stay focused on what he needed to do and not what had happened earlier.

He expelled a long, slow breath, dropped the folder on the desk and swiveled his chair around so that it faced the window.

She was out there. The tug of a smile arched his lips. All the circumstances that had led him to leave Louisiana and move to Atlanta weren't coincidences at all. Did she know? Did she believe as he did that they were destined to be together?

He pushed back from his chair and stood. Totally crazy, he thought as he shoved his papers back in his satchel and snapped it shut. Had someone told him he'd give up everything that was familiar and move to a new city in search of a woman he'd never seen before, he would have had them committed. But here he was.

Jackson opened the door and stepped out into the now busy corridor, teeming with eager young men and women bent on making a difference in the world. It was only a matter of time, he thought, before the two of them would meet again. He felt it in the marrow of his bones.

Just as he approached the entrance to his classroom, his teaching assistant, Victoria Rush, stopped him. Victoria was a doctoral student whose dissertation was on ancient and African art—his passion. She'd campaigned hard for the position and beat out several other candidates. Victoria was good. She was thorough and professional, but it was becoming clear to Jackson that Veronica spent a little too much time trying to prove herself to him. She always offered much more than the assignment called for, needing just a "few minutes" of his time a bit too often, even asking if there were any errands that he needed her to run.

On the surface it was all pretty harmless, but he was beginning to get an uncomfortable feeling. He hoped that this relationship wouldn't become a problem. Besides, one would think that her schedule would be pretty full without having to add his agenda to hers.

"Hey, Victoria, class is about to start."

"I know. I was hoping that I could talk to you after your class."

That uncomfortable feeling began with a tightness in his insides. "Is it the research paper?"

"Actually—" she lowered the books she was holding to her chest to reveal a low cut top "—it's personal."

"Personal? Victoria—Ms. Rush, if this has nothing to do with the course…"

"I know this may seem inappropriate, professor. But I don't know who else I can talk to." She blinked away the water that began to well in her eyes.

Aw, man. The last thing he needed was a crying grad student. "Okay, after class. Meet me in the cafeteria." At least the cafeteria was public.

She beamed a smile, flashing deep dimples in a nut-brown face. "Thank you." She turned and hurried away.

Jackson lowered his head for a second and blew out a frustrated breath then opened the classroom door. Hopefully his students would be awake, otherwise this was going to be a long hour and a half.

The ninety-minute Art History class wound down on an up note. The scheduled trip to the High Museum for the unveiling of the fertility statues was all set. The students actually seemed excited. Jackson left the class feeling good until he remembered his meeting with Victoria. Reluctantly he walked through the corridors until he reached the cafeteria. He couldn't imagine what Victoria could want or better, what he could do about it.

The tables were dotted with students huddled over textbooks and Styrofoam containers of French fries and half-eaten sandwiches. Jackson surveyed the brightly lit room and didn't see Victoria.

Deciding whether to duck out before she turned up, he started to leave and ran smack into her. Her books tumbled to the floor.

"I'll get that." Jackson bent down and so did Victoria, leaning provocatively over the tumble of books and loose papers.

"It's my fault. I shouldn't have walked up behind you like that," she said, gathering her papers into a neat pile.

Jackson picked up the two textbooks and stood. "Sorry about that." He looked around then back at her. "I've got to make this quick. I have another class."

"I know. It won't take long. Can we sit down for a minute?'

"Um, sure." He lifted his chin in the direction of an available table. "Over there."

"Great." She sauntered toward the table and sat down.

"So what did you want to talk about?" he asked, cutting to the chase. He set his briefcase on the floor near his feet.

"I know I've only been working with you for a short time, professor. And the experience has been wonderful. I enjoy the work and all the research." She paused. "But I'm going to have to give up my position," she blurted in one long breath.

Jackson didn't know if he should be relieved or annoyed. Victoria had practically begged her way into the position, one that didn't come easily to many grad students, especially women. With some urging from the search committee, he'd passed over several other equally qualified male prospects and finally settled on her.

"I see. Would you care to share your reason?"

She lowered her head for a moment. "It's personal." She reached across the table and covered his hand with hers with a beseeching look in her eyes right out of the soap operas. "Believe me, I don't want to go, but it's best." She pushed out a breath. "I'll finish up the project that I was working on for you and hand over all the notes."

"Victoria, are you sure you don't want to talk about it? Maybe I can help."

He watched her throat move and the words come up and then get swallowed. She pushed back from the table and stood. Then without another word she turned and nearly ran away. Several heads turned in her direction and then his. Questions hung in their eyes before they turned back to what they were doing.

Jackson sat there, not sure what had just happened. There was a part of him that was relieved but another part that left him with a bad feeling. Her entire demeanor had shifted in a little more than an hour. She hadn't given him any idea that she was planning to leave her position.

He shook it off, grabbed his briefcase and started out. Whatever her reason, he concluded, pushing through the glass door, it was probably for the best.

That last scene in the cafeteria was a little too dramatic for his taste. Meanwhile, he was going to have to find another assistant. He'd speak to the dean in the morning. Next time he was going to stick with his gut and get a guy.

Zoe hung up the phone with Sharlene. She'd booked her flight and said she was leaving her office early to do some shopping and go home and pack. They were all set to leave in the morning.

Zoe turned on her computer and reviewed the schedule. Mike would handle everything in her absence and assured her to take as much time as she needed. But the opening was in a week. She'd worked so hard to make it all happen and she wanted to be there. But if Nana Zora… Her mind wandered. She wouldn't think about that. Nana was going to be fine.

"Just hold on 'til I get there, Nana," she whispered.

Chapter 5

"Did you talk to your mom again?" Sharlene asked as they took their seats.

"I called last night. She said Nana was resting, still asking for me." She stuck her carry-on into the overhead compartment and slid into her window seat.

Sharlene followed suit. She grabbed Zoe's hand. "It's gonna be fine. Nana Zora is as tough as they come." She offered a reassuring smile.

"I know. My heart says that Nana will outlive us all. But reality is a different story, Sharl. She's been getting weaker year after year. She's ninety."

"Keep positive thoughts. Don't let your imagination run wild."

The pilot's easy drawl floated over the public address system. "Good morning. Welcome to Flight 1109 to New Orleans. I'm Captain Harris and I'll be your pilot today. The temperature in The Big Easy is a sultry 98 degrees." He chuckled. "And it's still early folks. We're third in line for takeoff, so sit back and relax and we'll be up in the air and back down again before you know it. Attendants, please prepare the cabin for takeoff."

Two blonde flight attendants strolled down the aisle, checking seat belts and telling passengers to put their seat backs upright. Moments later they were coasting down the runway then up in the air.

Zoe settled back and glanced out of the window watching the city of Atlanta grow smaller in the distance until the plane rose above the clouds and the earth disappeared.

"Speaking of imagination. I saw him," Zoe said.

"Huh?"

She turned in her seat. "I saw him. Actually saw him. Yesterday."

"What? Him, him? *The* him? Where? And why didn't you tell me?"

"It was yesterday morning and—"

"Yesterday!"

"Would you keep your voice down?" she hissed from between her teeth.

Sharlene looked around. "Why didn't you tell me?" she hissed right back.

"There was so much going on and I guess I

forgot." But she hadn't forgotten. Between worrying about her grandmother and preparing for her trip, her mind was on the man she'd met on 9th Street. She'd tried to convince herself that it was the stress of the moment, her feeling light-headed from the smoke. But her spirit told her differently and so did the dream she'd had. This time, her suitor, her lover was not a faceless man who teased and taunted her. It was him.

"So are you going to tell me what the hell happened or sit there staring with that silly grin on your face?"

Zoe blinked away the images and her gaze settled on Sharlene's face, with her lemon-puckered lips.

"Yesterday," she began. "I decided to walk to work…"

When she'd finished they both stared at each other in silence.

"Are you starting to believe, even just a little?" Sharlene asked.

Zoe breathed deeply. "I don't know what to believe. I mean, it's all so crazy, you know?" She gave a little laugh. "Destiny and legacy, and the man of your dreams come to life. Crazy." She reclined in her seat and stared out at the clouds. She propped her elbow on the armrest and pressed her fist to her mouth. "Crazy," she whispered.

Barely an hour later, flight 1109 was taxiing on the tarmac at Louis Armstrong International Airport.

"My mother said she'd meet us at baggage claim," Zoe said as they rode the escalator to the lower level.

"Mom still driving that big old Caddie?" Sharlene teased.

Zoe laughed. "You know she's not letting that thing go."

"How much gas do you think that bus guzzles?"

"Enough to pay off the national debt, especially at these prices."

"I know that's right."

"There she is. Ma!" Zoe called out and waved catching Miraya's attention.

At fifty-two, Miraya Beaumont was a stunning woman. She'd been mistaken for Lena Horne more times than she could count and still carried herself like the star she longed to be. Miraya had a string of suitors a mile long. And although she wasn't touring the country like she once did, she still sang in the lounges in the French Quarter.

Miraya took off her dark glasses and waved back.

Zoe instantly saw the heaviness in her mother's wide eyes and the waning of her smile. Her heart raced.

"Mom." She embraced her mother and realized for the first time how petite her mother was, fragile almost. Had she always been this thin? When had she seen her last—five, six months? She held her a moment longer then kissed her cheek. She stepped back and held her mother at arms length, searched her eyes. "Nana?"

Miraya's smile was tight. "She's hanging on." She took Sharlene's hand. "Good to see you, Sharl. It's been too long." She pulled her into an embrace. "How did you manage to get on a flight with such short notice?"

"I heard my family needed me," she said with a smile.

"Thanks for coming," she said softly. "Well, come on. Let's get you girls to the house and fix some breakfast. I know they didn't feed you on the plane."

They walked through the terminal to the airport garage arm in arm.

The short ride from the airport was spent in light conversation, and on the slow progress of rebuilding the Lower Ninth Ward. Much of the area had still not been rebuilt, as many residents had moved away along with their hopes of returning slowly fading.

Miraya pulled onto their street in the Garden District. Even in the early morning heat, neighbors were out and about, sweeping front porches or doing yard work, mostly because it was too hot to work as the day progressed.

"There's Ms. Ella," Zoe said, pointing to the octogenarian who knew everything about everybody on the street.

"The whole neighborhood will know you're home before the clock strikes nine," Sharlene teased.

"Be nice, girls," Miraya playfully warned as she pulled up and parked in front of the house.

The trio got out and Zoe and Sharlene took their bags from the trunk. "'Morning, Ms. Ella," they chorused and waved.

Ms. Ella pretended that she hadn't spotted them from the moment the big blue caddy came onto the street and craned her neck. She gave a delicate wave. "That you, Zoe?"

"Yes, ma'am," she called out.

"That Sharlene you got with you?"

"It's me, Ms. Ella."

She bobbed her wobbly head. "Zora's waiting for you," she said, her simple declaration carrying the weight they all held in their hearts.

The door of the row house on Sixth Street opened up and Zoe's aunts Flo and Fern stood in the doorway all dolled up in flowing, bright, floral-print caftans. The sisters were variations of the same face in shades of sandy brown to milk chocolate. It was the unpredictability of the genes, Nana Zora always said of her daughters.

Zoe's heart suddenly overflowed with emotion. The strain of caring for their ailing mother had taken its toll on her mother and aunts. Zoe could see it in their eyes. Yet, they still appeared formidable standing side by side against come what may.

Zoe hurried toward them, embracing both of them in her arms.

"Auntie," she whispered in each ear and against butter-soft cheeks.

"Welcome home, chile," Flo whispered.

"Come inside," Fern urged. She reached out her hand to Sharlene. "I knew you'd come."

The Beaumont women and their surrogate daughter went inside to see Nana.

From the front door of the two-story house, you could see straight through to the backyard, which was in full bloom thanks to the loving hands of Aunt Fern. Long, narrow windows with sheer white curtains filtered in the morning sunlight that reflected off of the oak floors. The furniture hadn't changed since the sisters were in their teens. Lovingly worn overstuffed armchairs were upholstered in a sea-green, brocade fabric, and antique, maple side tables with white doilies dotted the room. In the chair near the window, Nana Zora dozed as the rays of morning light warmed her face. Her lids fluttered and slowly opened. She turned her head. A slow smile spread across her face. "Zoe."

Zoe hurried across the room. She dropped her bag on the floor and knelt down beside her grandmother. She took her hands. "Nana."

"I knew you would come." Her eyes sparkled. She glanced around Zoe and saw Sharlene. "Come here and let me see you."

Sharlene did as she was told and knelt on the other side of the chair. "How are you doing, Nana?"

"Fine now that my Zoe is here." She patted Zoe's cheek. "And you, too, sugah," she said to Sharlene.

"Breakfast is ready," Aunt Flo called out.

"I'll bring your plate, Nana," Zoe said.

"Oh, no, you won't! I'm not an invalid," Zora insisted, as she seemed to regain her old strength in her voice. She reached for the cane propped up against her chair. Zoe grabbed her grandmother's elbow and helped her to her feet.

The three sisters moved back and forth between the stove and the round kitchen table bringing plates of fluffy eggs, fruit, sausage, bacon and grits.

"Let me help," Zoe insisted, taking a platter from her aunt Fern and bringing it to the table.

"Sharl, sweetie, would you get the juice from the fridge?" Miraya asked.

"Sure."

Finally, when everyone was settled at the table, the food was passed around and the plates were filled. They joined hands, bowed their heads and Nana Zora blessed the food.

"Thank you for this food and bless the hands that made it. Thank you for my family and for bringing Zoe home. Watch over her in the coming months, give her guidance and open her heart and her spirit to what will happen in the months to come. Amen."

Zoe opened her eyes and looked surreptitiously at her family.

"Amen," they chorused.

"How long can you stay?" Aunt Flo asked, directing her amber eyes at Zoe.

"As long as I need to."

"This will be a short visit," Nana said. "You have things to do."

"Nothing is more important than you, Nana Zora. Work can wait."

Nana waved a thin hand. "Yes, but not work in the way you mean. Rather the kind of work you need to do and you can't do it here."

All eyes turned to Zoe.

"I... I don't know what you mean."

"You will," said Aunt Fern.

"Let's eat, and leave that talk for later," interrupted Miraya. "You know how Zoe is about all that." She flashed her daughter a quick look of understanding.

"So what have I been missing around here? Are you ladies staying out of trouble?" Sharlene asked, changing the subject.

The sisters alternated telling stories about their neighbors, their new aches and pains and the changes in the world around them.

Nana Zora sat at the head of the table, observing her family like a queen on the throne. *There wasn't a lot of time,* she thought. She had so much to tell her granddaughter. Zoe needed to be prepared. Her own dreams were becoming stronger and she knew Zoe's were as well.

Her daughters were worried about her, about her health and her mental state. She wasn't slipping. Some days she simply preferred to live in the past, at the moment when things could have almost been different had she only used her gift. But she didn't. Now it was up to Zoe and the man who awaited her.

The glass of juice slid from her hand and onto the floor.

Everyone jumped up, practically tripping over each other, cleaning and wiping and checking on Nana.

"I'm tired," Nana said, her voice frayed and worn like an old housedress washed too many times.

Zoe's pulse leaped. "I'll take you to your room, Nana." She wrapped her arm around her grandmother's narrow waist and let her lean her nearly waiflike body against her own.

Zora's bedroom was on the first floor in the back of the house overlooking the garden. Zoe opened the bedroom door and led her grandmother across the room with the intention of putting her in bed.

"No, I want to sit by the window." With surprising strength she shook loose of Zoe's hold and walked unaided to the chair by the window. "Come sit near me," Nana said, patting the window seat next to her. "Close the door first. Don't want those nosy daughters of mine listening to what I need to tell you."

Zoe crossed the room, which always smelled of

baby powder, and closed the door. She came back and sat down on the window seat.

"Your birthday is soon."

"Yes. Three months."

"Seventy-eight days."

Zoe lowered her head and laughed. Only her grandmother knew exactly how many days until her thirtieth birthday. "Okay, seventy-eight days." She tucked her feet under her and let her gaze travel slowly over the history of her grandmother's face— from the thick silvery hair that hung in two braids down her back, her high forehead, thin arching brows, her wide, almond-shaped, all-knowing eyes, to the aquiline nose, high cheekbones and full lips. Zora Beaumont was still a stunning woman.

"You don't have much time. He's already here."

Zoe's pulse began to race.

"Isn't he?" Zora leaned forward.

"I…"

"You've seen him in your dreams." She smiled and looked off toward the garden. "It's how it begins you know. It happened with my mother and with me. It skipped right over my girls. But not you," she said, her voice taking on an air of storytelling. "You are the one. *The one,* Zoe."

Zoe leaned forward and clasped her grand-mother's hands. "The one to do what, Nana?"

"Fulfill the legacy, Zoe. Bring happiness back to the Beaumont women. He's been searching for you, too."

A shiver ran through her and the fine hairs on her arms tingled. "What do you mean he's been searching for me?" Her breath quickened.

Zora smiled. "I want you to open your mind and listen to me."

Zoe slowly nodded her head.

Zoe gently closed the bedroom door so as not to disturb her grandmother. She had been numbed by everything she'd heard. Although the story of the Beaumont women and the family legacy was something that had been talked about while she was growing up, she'd never really *heard* the story. She had listened to the tales of love between her great-great-grandparents who'd been torn apart and swore to find each other again. Zoe had always dismissed the stories as simply a romantic tragedy, one of many that happened during slavery. But she'd *heard* it this time, saw it in her mind, understood it and felt it in her heart in a way that changed her.

She felt light-headed and tired as if she'd been on a long journey. Maybe she had, she thought as she walked past her aunts in a daze. Her mother's and Sharlene's curious gazes followed her as she walked out the front door and sat on the porch steps.

She looked off, above the treetops that stood guard at the entrance to the house where her family lived.

The rational, analytic side of her, the part of her brain that dealt with facts and science, still struggled with the Beaumont part of her—the side that wanted to embrace the possibility of something spiritual. And maybe if she did, love would finally fill her life.

"Hey, you okay?"

Zoe glanced behind her. Sharlene stood in the doorway.

She gave a short mirthless laugh. "I don't know. I guess so."

Sharlene stepped out and sat beside Zoe. She put her arm around her friend's shoulder. "Did you at least have a good talk with Nana?"

"Nana did all the talking and she told me to go home and get ready." She twisted the end of her hair between her fingers. "This time I listened." She sighed. "I want to believe that there is someone out there that's just for me. But at the same time, I don't want to be the one responsible for my family's happiness. I don't want to have their future in my hands. I've seen what relationships have done to my family. Every one of them has loved and lost, tragically. Knowing that and witnessing their pain, I don't want it to be me." She looked at Sharlene, hoping to find understanding in her eyes.

Sharlene rested her head against Zoe's. "It won't be you, girl," she softly assured.

"Promise."

Sharlene pursed her lips and wished that she could promise happiness for her friend.

Chapter 6

Jackson strode out of Dean McRae's office more annoyed than when he'd walked in. The dean was a hundred years old if he was a day. He was hard of hearing and always wanted to talk about everything that was completely unrelated to the issue at hand. Jackson had spent the past half hour listening to Dean MacRae ramble on about growing up in Mississippi instead of what he'd come to discuss—getting a new teaching assistant.

"Hey, Jackson. What's up, man?"

Jackson slowed as Levi caught up with him in the hallway. "Hey. Just left McRae's office."

"Don't tell me. He told you the story of how he walked five miles to school each way, up a hill and barefoot," Levi said, chuckling.

Jackson grumbled. "Might as well have for all the good the conversation did me."

Levi clapped him on the shoulder. "Go talk to his assistant, Frank Miller. He's really the man behind the dean with the real power. McRae is a relic steeped in the college's past who they refuse to get rid of." He paused a moment. "Victoria ever say why she had to leave?"

"No. Just that it was personal."

"You did say she was making you a little nervous," Levi said as they walked into the teacher's lounge. "Probably the best thing that could've happened."

"Yeah," he muttered and poured a cup of coffee.

"You okay, man? You seem a little out of it." Levi reached for the milk.

"Mmm. A little tired. Didn't get much sleep last night."

Levi muttered knowingly. "Oh, I see."

Jackson gave him a look. "It's not what you think."

"You trying to tell me that you didn't sleep last night and it wasn't because a beautiful, sexy woman was keeping you up?"

"Right." Jackson started pouring sugar in his coffee. It was only partially true, he thought as he took a sip. It *was* a woman that kept him up—*the woman from the day of the fire.* Since he'd seen her and lost sight of her, he'd been driving himself crazy imagining that he saw her on every corner and in the faces of every woman who crossed his path in Atlanta. It had been a week and she was nowhere to be found.

"Got any plans for the weekend?" Levi leaned against the counter and sipped his coffee.

"I'm taking two of my classes to the opening at the High Museum tonight. Remember?"

Levi snapped his fingers. "Yeah, right. I've been so bogged down with this dissertation that I totally forgot. Mind if I tag along?"

Jackson grinned. "Nah, Not at all. We plan to meet in front of the humanities building at six, and then head over."

Levi nodded. "If I'm not out front, I'll meet you there. Maybe I'll get lucky and bring a date." He took another sip of his coffee. "I heard it's supposed to be a big opening, reporters, a fancy reception— the works." He tossed back the last of his coffee.

"It's kind of a big deal to finally get those statues here. I'm anxious to see them up close myself." He put his empty cup in the sink.

"You believe in all that mumbo jumbo about the statues?"

Jackson's brows flickered. "You mean all that fertility stuff?"

Levi nodded. "Yeah."

Jackson shrugged. "Who knows? I guess people can be convinced of anything if you tell the same story often enough." *Like he was becoming convinced about his destiny,* he thought. Not so much by the things he had been told, but by the visions, the dreams and the inexplicable reasons that brought him to Atlanta. "Anything is possible," he murmured.

The museum was closed for the day in preparation for the exhibit opening and reception later that evening. The maintenance crew was in full force polishing and shining every surface in the massive building.

"Right, three cases," Zoe replied, as she held the phone. She massaged her temples. Her head was pounding. She hadn't slept a wink and exhaustion weighed heavily on her lids. "Yes, I need them here no later than noon. They should have been here yesterday. Thank you. Noon." She hung up the phone and rested her head in her hands.

Dealing with the wine delivery was only the third thing on her list of more than a dozen things on her checklist to take care of in the next few hours. The caterer had delivered the wrong tables and set-up and had to return them to the catering hall and deliver the right set-up and food in only a few hours. Two of her staff had called in sick with the flu, and Mike and Linda had gotten into a shouting match in the inventory room. She'd had to send Linda out on a break and have a heart-to-heart with Mike.

She'd never felt so unnerved and rattled before. Everything seemed to be making her jumpy, taking on mammoth proportions. She'd hosted plenty of museum opening receptions before, so that wasn't it. Drawing in a deep breath she could actually feel her insides flutter.

It had been like that for the entire week since she'd returned from New Orleans. She couldn't shake off her thoughts about the things her grandmother had confided in her. If anything, her feelings about what she'd been told about her family and her own future had only intensified.

She could almost say his name now. It hung on the tip of her tongue, but was always just out of reach. His scent often teased her, surprising her with its suddenness, especially in strange places like when she opened her closet door or walked into an empty room, or leafed through the pages of a novel.

He's already here. The prophecy echoed in her ear and Zoe could no longer deny it. One of the few things she was certain of, was that the man she saw on the day of the fire was her destiny—the key that would unlock the past and free the Beaumont family from generations of heartache. Why hadn't she asked him his name? How would she ever find him again?

The short rap on her partially opened door pulled her back to reality. Mike stood in the doorway.

Zoe pushed out a breath. "Yes?"

"Mind if I come in?"

"Actually, I do, but come in anyway."

At least he had the decency to look sheepish, she

thought and wondered if she should have taken an Aleve for her headache before it got much worse. "What's up?"

Mike pulled up a chair and sat down. There was no denying it, Mike Williams was a gorgeous man and she could see why Linda made herself so crazy. However, he wouldn't give her the time of day.

"I wanted to apologize again about what happened this morning. I shouldn't have let it get that far."

Zoe leaned back a bit in her chair and looked him straight in the eye. "No, you shouldn't have. We've been down this road before, Mike. I rely on you when I'm not here. And when I'm not, I can't be concerned that World War Three is going to break out." She shook her head in frustration. "You're going to have to find a way to work it out, Mike. Both of you are important members of this team."

"Believe me I've tried. Some days things are fine and then others…turn out like this morning." He lowered his head momentarily. "I don't get it." He looked up at Zoe.

I do, she thought but refrained from saying. Linda was in love with him. You could see it in her eyes and the way her whole body lit up when he walked into a room. Sometimes she wondered what that was like, to feel that strongly about someone. But then again, look at what it got Linda—nothing but heartache and frustration. That's not what she wanted in her life. Every example she'd had in life had proven over and over again that love hurt.

Mike stood up from his seat, snapping Zoe back to attention. "I'll make it work. Maybe I should take her to lunch and have a talk."

"Hmm, I don't know if that would be a good move. You don't want her to get the wrong idea. Maybe coffee in the employee lounge or something?"

"Yeah, that makes sense." He shoved his hands into his pockets. "Ready for tonight?"

"Pretty much. If I can just get these vendors to make their deliveries, I'd be fine."

"Let me know if you need anything."

"I will. Oh, if you can call the security company and make sure that everything is taken care of, confirm how many people they are giving us, and if they can cover the front of the building as well. We're expecting a big crowd this evening and I don't want any mishaps."

"No problem."

"Thanks."

Linda appeared at the door just as Mike turned to leave.

They muttered their apologies and made a mess of stepping around each other. Zoe tried not to laugh. Those two just needed to get together and call it a day.

"Yes, Linda."

Linda Gilmore was what her aunties would call

"bright-skinned." Back in the day she could have probably passed. Her light brown eyes were sometimes green depending on the weather and her mood. Her sleek hair hung in light waves around her shoulders framing a nearly perfectly oval face. She was a Pilates devotee and it showed in her long, lean body. And she was smart. Linda was definitely the whole package. Too bad Mike didn't see it.

"There's a reporter here from one of the local papers. He wants to speak with you."

"This early? The museum isn't even open."

"Guess he wanted to get a scoop. What do you want me to tell him?"

"I'll come out and talk to him. Thanks."

They exited Zoe's office and walked down the corridor together.

"You feeling a little better?" Zoe asked.

Linda's cheeks flushed. "I'm good." She gave a tight-lipped smiled.

Zoe stopped and gently clasped Linda's arm. "Listen, whatever it is that is going on or not going on between you and Mike has got to stop. It's interfering with work, with scheduling, other staff members and I can't have that. We're all adults here and this can't be the place for drama. I don't want some other staffers to complain to human resources. Then we will really have a problem and it'll be out of my hands."

Linda started to protest. Zoe held up her hand.

"I'm not saying it's all you. I've told Mike pretty

much the same thing, too. Both of you are important members of this team. But I'm going to have to think of some other alternative if we can't find a compromise."

Linda's lips pinched and her eyes filled with water. "You know what it's like to love someone and they don't even see you?" she blurted out then turned her head away. "I'm sorry." Linda pulled away and walked off.

Zoe stood there for several moments. This whole love thing was totally overrated, she thought. Is this what was in store for her? If so, she didn't want any parts of it—legacy or not. She turned down the corridor toward the entrance to meet the reporter.

Her heels clicked with precision against the marble floors. The young reporter was seated on a bench under a piece of art from Ghana, Zoe's ancestor's homeland. It was one of her favorites, with its vibrant colorful beading depicting a small village at night set against the backdrop of towering mountains and greenery. She extended her hand as she approached.

"I'm Zoe Beaumont. How can I help you?"

The young man stood. He couldn't have been more than twenty-five, Zoe surmised. He shook her hand.

"Gabe Weston from *The Eagle*. Thank you for seeing me."

"You do know that the exhibit doesn't open until tonight."

"Yes, but I was hoping to get a jump on the competition," he said, flashing a killer smile.

Zoe's right brow arched. She held back a grin. "Really? Well, other than the catalogues that everyone else is getting, I'm not sure what I can offer you."

"I was hoping you would allow me to ask a few questions."

"You want to interview me?"

"Yes. It will only take five minutes. I promise."

Zoe looked around then focused back on him. "Sure. Five minutes." She sat down on the bench and he pulled out a tape recorder and sat beside her.

"I have what I need about the statues. What I want to know from you is why was it important to bring them here?"

"As a curator you are always searching for pieces that will bring in visitors and provide them with the opportunity to experience treasures from around the world. I spend a great deal of my time looking for pieces of art and sculptures. Of course it brings a great deal of prestige and exposure to the museum to house one-of-a-kind pieces and artifacts."

"And how do you make your decisions?"

She smiled. "My passion, and the budget."

He laughed.

"Speaking of budgets, the arts are always hit hardest during any economic downturns. How has the economy affected the museum?"

Zoe blew out a breath. "It's certainly been

difficult. Part of what I do is write grants, try to get corporate sponsors and museum patrons to help, and tonight's event is also a fundraiser. Those things help to offset some of the costs, but not all of them."

"What do you want readers to know?"

She was thoughtful for a moment. "Museums are home to countless treasures. They are not only a source of entertainment and knowledge, but also enlightenment about culture and art. They tell so many stories that would be otherwise lost. They are places where the average person can travel to any corner of the world and learn its history."

"How long did it take you to get the statues here?"

"It was a long process. Almost two years."

"Do you believe the stories about the statues?"

"It's not for me to believe or disbelieve, just to present and let the visitors decide for themselves. Everyone who comes here or to any museum takes away something."

"Well, if there is a mini baby-boom in the next year, I guess Atlanta might have you to thank. If you believe in that kind of stuff."

Zoe stood. "I really have to get back to work. I have a full day."

He turned off the tape recorder and stood. "Thank you for your time, Ms. Beaumont."

"Will you be here tonight?"

"Absolutely."

"I'll make sure you get some good photos."

"Thanks. I'd really appreciate that."

"Security will see you out."

"Thanks again."

Zoe nodded, turned away and headed back toward her office. About halfway there, she took a detour and took the elevator downstairs to where the statues were still under wraps.

Several members of the maintenance team were unloading crates when she came in. She walked through the cavernous space among the paintings and sculptures, boxes and crates until she reached the room where the statues were being held. She punched in the security code on the panel and the door buzzed open.

The instant she walked in the room, her skin began to tingle and the scent—his scent wrapped around her. She drew in a long, deep breath and her heart began to race. She gripped the head of the female statue to keep from falling and what seemed like a spark of electricity shot through her arm. She jerked her hand away and backed out of the room, practically running all the way to her office.

Chapter 7

After his last class, Jackson went home to shower and change, and grab a quick bite to eat. He'd been to his share of receptions, and food wasn't high on the list of reasons to attend. He barely had two hours to get ready and back to campus. He pulled up in front of his building and noticed someone sitting on his front steps. *Victoria*. What the… Something told him to keep on driving, but time was not on his side. He had a bad feeling.

He pulled into his driveway, shut off the engine and willed himself to be calm. How did she even know where he lived? Reluctantly he got out and slowly approached. Victoria stood.

"I know I shouldn't be here," she said before he could get a word out. "But I had to see you."

Jackson took a quick look around. "Victoria, this is not cool. Whatever you need to talk to me about we can do on campus or during my office hours."

"I know. But…please listen." She took a step forward and reached a hand toward his chest.

Jackson eased back and gave them some distance. "I'm listening."

Victoria lowered her arm. "I wanted to tell you the real reason why I stopped working as your assistant."

"Okay. What was the reason?"

"Some people who you think are in your corner aren't."

Jackson let out a breath of frustration. "What are you talking about?"

"You're up for chair of your department."

"Yes," he said with a hint of caution in his voice.

"There are some people that don't want you to have it."

He frowned. "And you know this how?"

"It was no accident that I got assigned to you or that I petitioned so hard for the spot."

"What exactly are you trying to tell me, Victoria?"

"Professor Treme, no matter what you do, you won't get that position. My real job was to spy on you, to pass along information about you and your research."

"To whom?"

"I can't tell you that. What I can tell you is to watch your back. Everyone is not who they make themselves out to be. I like you, professor. I think that you're an incredible teacher and I just couldn't be a part of it anymore. And please, don't tell anyone I told you this. I'm putting in for a transfer for next semester. But if they found out that I said anything. I have a lot on the line, too."

"I...don't know what to say. This is crazy."

"I've got to go." She started off.

"Victoria...wait."

She stopped and turned.

"Thank you."

She gave him a half smile and hurried toward her beige Honda that was parked at the curb.

Jackson watched her drive away, almost rooted to the spot. He shook his head. It didn't make sense. Why go through all that trouble? Better yet, who would go through all that trouble?

His cell phone rang shaking him out of his troubling thoughts. He pulled the phone from his pocket. Levi's number lit up the digital face. "Hey, what's up?"

"Yeah, I wanted to let you know that I'll probably meet you at the museum. I got kind of tied up." He chuckled.

"Hmm, okay."

"See you later."

"Yeah. Sure."

"Hey, everything cool?"

"Yeah, everything's fine," he said absently, as Victoria's warning played in his head. *Everyone is not who they make themselves out to be.* Did that include Levi? "I'm just walking into my place," he added. "Gotta get a move on."

"Cool. See you later."

"Sure. Later." He disconnected the call and shoved the phone back into his pocket. He checked his mailbox, took out three bills then stuck the key into the lock of his front door and opened it.

He set his briefcase down on the console table in the entry hallway and went into the kitchen to see what he could throw together quickly. He washed his hands at the sink then searched through the fridge. He had some leftover chicken and decided to make himself a sandwich, which he took upstairs.

Between bites he undressed and took a shower. The conversation with Victoria was still playing in his head. Who was she talking about?

He stepped out of the shower and into his bedroom. He barely had an hour left before he had to meet the students. Opening his closet door, he took out his black shirt and black slacks. The temperature was in the high eighties, but he planned to wear a jacket anyway. He took his sports jacket out and put everything on the bed and started to get dressed just as the doorbell rang.

"Now what?" He wasn't up for any more surprises. He pulled on his pants and shoved his arms in his shirt and went downstairs to the door and pulled it open. "Michelle! What in the world…?"

"I know I should have called…"

His surprise shifted to alarm when he focused on her stricken expression then to his niece, Shay, who stood at her side. He scooped up his five-year-old niece. "Hey, sweetie." He glanced at his sister over Shay's head, put his arm around Michelle's shoulder and ushered her inside.

Jackson set his niece down then stooped down to her level. "Look how big you are."

She giggled. "We came to visit, Uncle Jack."

"So I see. And I'm glad you're here. I was getting lonely for my favorite niece." He grinned and kissed her head.

Shay spotted his giant television. "Can I watch *Dora the Explorer?* Please, Uncle Jack."

"Sure, sweetie." He turned on the television, surfed to the channel guide and found the cartoon.

Shay settled back on the couch and within moments was totally engrossed in her favorite show.

Jackson turned to Michelle. "Let's go in the kitchen," he said softly. She followed him. "Can I get you anything?"

"Some water or juice will be fine," she said, her voice sounding hollow. She lowered herself into the chair at the table.

Jackson opened the fridge and took out a container of apple juice and poured her a glass. He set it in front of her and sat down. "What happened, Mikki?"

She blinked rapidly to hold back the tears she'd kept at bay during the hours-long drive from New Orleans. "I left him."

"What?" He lurched forward. "Travis? What in the world happened?"

"I came home…early yesterday. I wasn't feeling well and…"

Jackson's pulse started to pound. *Don't let her say what I think she's going to say.*

"He…she…he was in bed with Carla."

Time froze and the room seemed to vibrate. What she'd said didn't make sense. Carla and Travis? "Michelle…he was with Carla?"

She nodded silently and then the tears came in a downpour, silent and loud all at once. And Jackson felt every iota of her heartache twist and turn inside of him.

He came around the table, knelt beside her and gathered her in his arms. "Let it out," he encouraged. "I'm here. It's going to be all right."

"I had nowhere else to go. I couldn't stay there in that house where they…"

He gently stroked her back. "It's okay. My home is yours and Shay's for as long as you need it." He held her tighter, trying to put the horrible scenario together in his head. His thoughts spun out of control. Travis and Carla—his ex…

"Oh, God," she moaned. "How could he do this

to me? How?" Deep wracking sobs shook her body. "And Carla…"

All Jackson could see was red. He was going to hurt Travis. He was going to pay.

"What's wrong, Mommy?"

Jackson's head jerked up. Michelle swiped at her eyes and forced a smile on her face before she turned around.

"Nothing, baby. I'm just tired from that long drive." She swallowed and sniffed.

Shay stood in the doorway, her innocent brown eyes looking from her mother to her uncle.

"Why don't you go up and rest for a while, I'll get Shay something to eat."

Michelle rushed to her feet. "I'll be right upstairs if you need me," she said, her voice still shaky. She stroked Shay's braids and walked out looking as if she'd aged ten years.

"Mommy's sad," Shay said.

"A little bit. But she will be fine."

"I don't like it when Mommy's sad."

"I know, sweetheart. Neither do I. So that's why you have to be extra sweet to her until she feels better. Okay?"

Shay bobbed her head.

"Now," he said lifting her up and bracing her on his hip. "What would you like?"

"Ice cream!"

Jackson chuckled. "Ice cream it is."

* * *

Once Jackson had gotten Shay settled, he went upstairs to check on his sister. He found her curled in a tight knot in the center of the guestroom bed. He sat down on the side.

Michelle opened her eyes, which were now red and swollen. "I must look a mess," she murmured and pushed her hair away from her face. She focused on her brother. "You're dressed to go out." She sat up. "Jack, I didn't even realize... I just came barging in..."

"Mikki, take it easy. It's okay. Relax. It's the opening at the museum that I was telling you about. I'm taking my class. But I can call my assistant..." He remembered he didn't have an assistant anymore. "I can make some calls and tell them to go on without me."

"No, absolutely not! Shay and I will be fine."

"Look, why don't I take Shay with me so that you can get some rest?"

She was pensive for a moment. "Are you sure? You know how wound up she can get sometimes."

"Don't worry about it. We'll be fine."

"At least let me clean her up and change her clothes." She scooted off the bed.

"Michelle..."

She turned.

"It's going to be all right. Understand?"

She nodded and hurried out.

Jackson stood in the center of the room. Rage

burned inside him. It took all of his willpower not to jump in his car and head straight to New Orleans. However, he had to think of his sister and his niece first. But Travis was going to pay.

Chapter 8

Jackson and twenty-five of his students stood in the long line to enter the museum. Twilight was approaching and the spotlights that moved in slow arcs above and around the buildings gave the evening a real Hollywood feel.

The arriving crowd was dressed for a major opening, in business suits and gowns to sparkling jewelry and tuxedos. Jackson was glad he'd decided on the jacket even though he'd decided not to wear a tie.

"This is a pretty big deal, huh, Professor Treme?" one of his students commented while adjusting his tie.

"Looks that way."

"Will we be able to take pictures?" another young lady asked him.

"I'm not sure. They'll let us know once we get inside."

"Why are all these people here, Uncle Jack?"

Jackson looked down at Shay. "They all came to see the special statues."

She frowned in confusion for a minute. "Why?"

Jackson chuckled. "Because they're special."

Shay blinked. "Oh. Like me?"

"Yep. Just like you." He squeezed her hand. "Now remember what we talked about. No wandering. You hold my hand. Okay?"

"Okay."

They inched along the line, showing their passes at the entrance and finally they were inside.

The rotunda of the museum was awash in lights and activity. White-jacketed waiters circulated among the throng with platters of tempting hors d'œuvres and canapés. Photographers took pictures of those attending the opening and the statues themselves. There was a low hum of excitement and conversation that buzzed in the air.

"Take good notes," he told his students before they dispersed into pairs and groups of threes.

"Is that the special statue?" Shay asked, pointing to a terracotta figure of an elegant African figure from the ancient city of Djenne, in Mali.

"No, sweetheart." He walked her closer to the sculpture and read the description below it.

"Then where are they? I'm hungry."

Jackson chuckled. "Okay. One thing at a time. Let's get you some food first and then we'll go find the special statues."

Shay enthusiastically bobbed her head and skipped beside her uncle while Jackson led them around the bodies to the long buffet table. As he was selecting what he thought she would like, a warm sensation began to flow through him. His stomach clenched and he had the overwhelming sensation that someone was sneaking up on him. He spun around only to see a room full of well-dressed people. His pulse raced like crazy. A flashbulb went off to his left. He turned and there she was. It was her—the woman from the fire, from his dreams. The paper plate fell from his hand.

"Uncle Jack!" Shay whined, tugging on his jacket. "You dropped all the food."

"I'll get that sir." A young woman dressed in all black, obviously one of the catering staff, began to clean it up.

In the flurry of activity Jackson looked back to where he'd seen her, and she was gone and the room seemed to have exploded with even more people.

Jackson let go of an expletive that was muffled when the five-piece band began to play. He tried to peer over the heads of the guests to see if he could spot her. It was as if he'd only imagined her. But he hadn't, he was sure of it.

"What's wrong, Uncle Jack?"

He shook off his frustration and focused on

Shay's upturned face. He smiled. "Uncle Jack is just a little crazy today," he said, only half joking. "Let me try fixing you another plate and then we'll go find the statues."

As he selected the canapés and crudités, adding them to Shay's plate, he scanned the room as best he could. Where had she gone?

"Let's go over to that bench so you can sit down and eat."

"Don't spill it this time Uncle Jack, 'cause I'm really hungry."

Jackson hustled Shay into a spot and got her settled. He wanted to tell her to just gobble it down so that he could continue searching for the woman. Every nerve ending in his body was on edge. His foot tapped out a nervous beat. Shay was eating each piece of food with the speed of a snail. He couldn't sit still and jumped up, pacing the square foot of space in front of them, all the while peering in between bodies and over heads.

"Finished!"

Jackson glanced at Shay who was holding out her half-eaten plate of food. "I thought you were starving," he teased, and took her plate.

She hopped up from the bench. "I was."

"Okay. Come on, let's go find those statues."

"What an amazing turnout," Mike said, walking alongside Zoe.

"I can't believe it. I guess all that PR work we've been doing paid off."

"Yes, in dollars," he said laughing. "It will definitely help to close the budget gap." He glanced at her. "You look amazing tonight," he said in a tone that caused Zoe to shoot him a look. He was staring down at her with a smile that was a hairsbreadth short of inviting.

A nervous flutter jumped in her stomach. "Thank you," she said over a smile. "You don't look too bad yourself," she added, lightly poking him in the arm, hoping to defuse the heat that danced in his eyes.

He placed his hand at the small of her back as they moved through the crowd. Zoe stiffened ever so slightly. "I'm going to see if I can find Sharlene. Keep mingling," she said and hurried off in the opposite direction. What was that about? she wondered as she smiled and greeted people in the crowd. She'd reached the archway leading into one of the exhibit rooms when she nearly tumbled over a little girl. Righting herself she caught the child's shoulder to keep her from tumbling backward.

"Oh, my goodness, I'm so sorry, sweetheart. I didn't see you. Are you okay?" she asked bending down to eye level. Tears ran down the child's cheeks. "Did I hurt you? Where's your mom?" She looked over the child's head then back at her when she didn't notice anyone rushing to her aid.

"She's not here," she whimpered. "I'm in big trouble."

"Who did you come with?"

"My uncle."

"Do you know where your uncle is?"

She shook her head no.

"Okay." Zoe stood and exhaled a breath. She looked around. How could someone be so irresponsible? The museum was too crowded not to be paying attention to a child.

"What's your uncle's name, sweetheart?"

"Uncle Jack."

Zoe bit back a smile. "We'll find Uncle Jack in no time. Okay?" She took Shay's hand. "Let's go to the security desk."

Shay dug in her heels and pulled away. "My mommy said not to go with strangers." She started crying again.

"But I'm not…you're right. And your mommy is right. Um…" She looked around, raised up on tip-toe to see if she could spot one of the security guards. Now she wished she hadn't listened to Sharlene when she said that the walkie-talkie clashed with her black-beaded cocktail dress. She looked great, but she couldn't communicate with the staff and her purse was locked in her desk along with her cell phone. "Frank!" she called out, turning several heads in her direction. "Frank." She waved her hand above her head. Finally he saw her and wound his way over.

Frank Monroe was her chief of security. "Hey, Ms. Beaumont. What can I do for you?"

"This young lady is lost. Could you get on the intercom and let Uncle Jack know that we found his niece…" She bent down to Shay. "What's your name, sweetie?"

"My mommy said not to tell strangers my name." She blinked rapidly.

Zoe and Frank shared a look.

"Do you know your uncle Jack's last name?"

She slowly shook her head no.

Zoe pushed out a breath. "Okay, Frank. Get on the intercom and ask for 'Uncle Jack.' We have his niece in front of the American Arts wing."

"No problem."

All Jackson could imagine was the worst. He tore in and out and around the thousands of people who had filled the museum. It was a split second and she was gone. The museum was humongous in size with several floors and adjacent building. *Oh, my God.* He had to find someone in charge.

"May I have your attention?" A smooth modulated voice came through the intercom system. "Would *Uncle Jack* please come to the entrance to the American Arts wing on the second floor."

Jackson stopped in his tracks.

"Uncle Jack," he repeated, "Please come to the second floor. The American Arts wing."

"Thank God." He darted toward the stairs, taking them two at a time, barely avoiding knocking people over. He reached the landing and looked around frantically for the American Arts wing. He saw the signage and jogged down the corridor when suddenly he felt as if someone had slammed him in the chest. The air lodged in his lungs.

It was her.

Zoe felt him before she saw him, like a hand stroking her bare flesh. Her pulse quickened and heat infused her veins. She turned and there he was. Their gazes connected like lightning hitting a tree and the entire room brightened.

The crowd, of its own volition, seemed to part leaving them an open path toward each other.

Jackson moved, dreamlike toward her, as everything around them receded. All he could see was her.

"Hello, again," he said, a melodiousness lacing his voice. He wanted to touch her to convince himself that she was real.

"Hello." She looked up into his eyes that were darker than eternity and lost herself there.

"Uncle Jack!" Shay buried her face against his thigh. "Please don't tell mommy."

Jackson shook himself out of the trance that he was in and scooped Shay up into his arms, kissing her cheeks in relief. He held her close but couldn't take his eyes off of Zoe. He wouldn't dare. "Thank you."

"Of course," she said a bit breathless.

"Jackson. Jackson Treme."

"Zoe Beaumont."

For a moment all they could do was stare at each other. No words could convey the tumultuous thoughts that swirled through their heads. The stories, the myths, the dreams, the hopes and fears all warred inside their heads for attention.

"I'm here with my class," Jackson finally said.

"Oh." Zoe snapped to attention. "Class?"

"Yes, I'm a professor at Clarke-Atlanta."

"Really? What do you teach?"

"Art history, mainly."

"I work here. I'm the head curator for the African History Museum."

He laughed, thinking of all the times he'd walked past the museum and she'd been there all along engrossed in the very thing he loved—history. A part of him seemed to know that it couldn't have been any other way and couldn't have happened at any time other than now. Was it possible that she was even more beautiful than he remembered from their brief encounter?

She watched the light dance in his eyes and the way the curves around his luscious lips deepened when he smiled revealing beautiful, even teeth. She wanted to stroke the strong jaw and run her finger along the line of his brow, touch the small scar there and ask him how it happened. But she knew. Somehow she knew that it happened when he was about twelve and he'd been riding his bike down a hill and he hit a rock and went flying. She also knew that one day he would tell her all about it.

"Have you seen the exhibit yet?" she managed to ask.

"No. That's what we were on our way to do when…we got separated." He squeezed Shay a bit tighter against him.

"I'd be happy to show you."

"I'd like that."

They walked side by side, intermittently stealing glances and sharing smiles of amazement at each other. And it felt perfect, natural, as if walking together was something that they'd always done.

"Zoe…" He loved the way her name rolled off his tongue, and vibrated down to his center.

"Yes?"

"Have you ever met someone for the first time but felt that you've known them all your life?"

Zoe stopped walking and gazed up at him. "Yes." Her eyes moved in increments across his face and her polished lips moved into a smile that expressed more than any words ever could. Coming from anyone else she would have dismissed it as a come on line, but not Jackson Treme. He wasn't like other men. He was her destiny.

Jackson had the urgent need to touch her to discover if her skin was a silky as it appeared. He wanted to take her in his arms and rest his head against her neck and inhale her scent, mold her against his body. He wanted to let go of the dream and capture reality. He wanted to know everything about her, listen to her tell him about her life, which he had been led to become a part of. All that would come in time. Of that he was certain.

"There you are." Mike approached, short-circuiting the electricity that popped between them. "I've been looking all over. I called you on the two-way."

"Oh, I left it in the office."

Mike looked at Jackson and realizing that they were together his expression stiffened.

"Mike, this is Jackson Treme. Mr. Treme, Mike Williams, assistant curator."

Jackson shifted Shay in his arms and stuck out his hand. "Pleasure."

"Enjoying the exhibit?"

"We were actually heading into the main attraction."

Mike peered around Jackson's shoulder. "Looks like your little girl is out for the count." He chuckled.

"No wonder she got so heavy." He stroked her back. "My niece."

Mike snapped his fingers. "You're Uncle Jack!"

"Guilty."

"Yeah, gotta be careful with kids. They can get away from you." Mike turned his full attention on Zoe. "The chairman is here. He wanted to speak to you."

Zoe's eyes widened. "Chairman Lang? Where is he?"

"On the first floor in the lounge."

She turned to Jackson. "It was really nice to meet you."

"And you. Thanks. About Shay…"

She waved off his thanks. "Not a problem."

He wanted to ask when he could see her again, but he could feel the testosterone exuding from Mike in waves and wondered if their relationship went beyond work.

"Professor! Professor, over here," one of his students called out and waved him over to where the group had assembled.

"Duty calls."

"Yes, it does. Enjoy your evening," Zoe said and walked off with Mike.

Jackson watched her until she was hidden by the crowd then he went to join his students. He knew where she was now. That was all that mattered. *Zoe Beaumont*.

Chapter 9

Zoe felt like she was disconnected from her body, yet every fiber of her being seemed more alive than ever before. Colors were more vivid. The lights were brighter. She could hear the air move through the building. There was an inexplicable happiness inside of her that made her want to weep with joy and dance to silent music.

She wasn't even sure what Chairman Lang was saying to her. She simply smiled and nodded at what she thought were all the appropriate places. But her mind was with Jackson Treme. That's what she wanted to tell everyone. Jackson Treme. He wasn't a dream. He was real. He was flesh and blood and gorgeous and…

"Ms. Beaumont…"

Zoe blinked, snapping out of her daydream and focused on Chairman Lang. She smiled sweetly.

"What do you think about that?" David Zuckerman, a board member from New York asked.

"Think about that…?"

"Yes. The Guggenheim?"

She was at a total loss. "I'm sorry. I have so much on my mind. Can you repeat that?"

He cleared his throat and looked at her askance. "As I was saying, if tonight's results are as spectacular as we believe they are, we'd like you to spend three months in New York at the Guggenheim to mount a fall show."

She gave a quick shake of her head. "Excuse me?"

"It's the opportunity of a lifetime," Phil Harris, one of the High's board members, said.

"But…"

Lang held up his hand and chuckled. "I know it's a lot to take in. You wouldn't have to leave right away, of course. Think about it and we'll talk in a week or so."

Talk in a week or so? She was speechless. How did the conversation go from zero to one hundred in the blink of an eye?

In a daze, she got up from her seat and glanced around the room at the smiling faces. Did they just offer her a job at the Guggenheim?

"Congratulations," Lang said enthusiastically.

"Enjoy your evening," she murmured and walked away. She stepped into the corridor and Mike was there waiting.

"Everything cool? You look shaken."

"Yes, everything is fine," she said in a faraway voice and kept walking. It was a dream assignment. She should be ecstatic. If this had been any other time, she would be. *Now*. Why now?

She slowly walked down the wide, winding staircase and stood for a moment looking out at the activity below. She wouldn't begin to guess how many people had attended tonight's event. And from where she stood, the board was right, it was a success and they had her and her team to thank. She continued down the stairs, her thoughts a jumbled mess that shuffled back and forth between tonight's event, her family, her grandmother, meeting Jackson and now the Guggenheim Museum. She couldn't think straight. She needed some space, some quiet and some time to think and sort things out.

The reception would be over in an hour. Sharlene had promised to meet up in Zoe's office at the end of the night. Sharl was the only person she could talk to…about everything.

Jackson lifted Shay from the backseat of the Explorer and carried her into the house. Michelle was resting on the couch and jumped up when they came through the door. She hurried over to him.

"I'll take her."

"No, she's too heavy for you to carry her up the stairs."

"Fine, but I do it all the time."

She followed them upstairs and once Jackson had put Shay on the bed, Michelle gently began to get her daughter undressed, miraculously completing the task without waking her.

"Can you hand me her nightgown? It's on the chair."

Jackson walked to the corner of the bedroom and picked up the pink nightgown. Shay's favorite cartoon character, *Dora the Explorer,* was emblazoned on the front. Jackson smiled then handed Michelle the gown.

"I met her tonight."

Michelle stopped what she was doing and whipped her head in Jackson's direction. "What?" she said in a hot whisper. Her eyes were wide with surprise. "The same woman you told me about from the day of the fire?"

Jackson nodded and leaned against the dresser. "Her name is Zoe Beaumont. She's the curator at the museum."

Michelle gently lifted her daughter's head, slid the gown over it and then put her arms through the sleeves. She put Shay under the covers and gave her a tender kiss good-night.

Shay stirred then settled under the light blanket.

Michelle eased off the bed and she and Jackson tiptoed out.

She took his hand and looked up into his eyes. "Are you sure?" she asked in an urgent whisper.

He nodded. "Yes, I am."

She tugged on her bottom lip with her teeth, her own troubles forgotten. "Tell me. Tell me everything. What's she like? Is she cute?"

Jackson tossed his head back and laughed. "Very cute. Come on downstairs. I'll fix us a drink."

They held hands going down the stairs just like they used to do when they were kids, and the realization simultaneously hit them. They looked at each other and chuckled.

"I have some raspberry rum," said Jackson.

"Add a little coke and some ice and I'm good."

"Yes ma'am."

Michelle curled up in the side chair. "Soooo, what is she like?"

Jackson handed Michelle her drink then sat down opposite her on the couch. "She's stunning for starters."

Michelle grinned. "Of course you would say that. What else?"

"Well, it's kind of hard to describe. She's..." He trailed off, then frowned for a moment searching for the right words. "She's everything. That's the only way I can put it." He looked at his sister, hoping that she would understand what he couldn't explain. "Her voice. Her eyes. Her spirit." How could he put into words that someone whom he'd only imagined to be real actually was?

"When are you going to see her again?"

He sipped his drink. "We didn't get that far."

"Huh?"

"Let me start from the beginning." He told her about the feeling he had at the museum and carefully told her about losing Shay and that it was Zoe who found her.

Her mouth opened then closed it. "Shay got lost?" she finally said.

"Sis, I'm sorry. It happened so fast. One minute she was there and then she wasn't. I…"

"It's okay. She's safe. She wasn't hurt. That's what's important." She paused a moment. "You know how Grandma used to always say that everything happens for a reason?"

"Yeah?"

She let out a slow breath. "As awful as my reason for being here is, maybe we were supposed to be here today. Shay was supposed to get lost so that you two could find each other." Her eyes filled and she turned her head away. She pressed her fist to her mouth.

"Mikki…" He sprung up from his seat and squeezed in beside her in the chair. He put his arm around her and pulled her close.

"I'm sorry," she whimpered. "You should be celebrating." She rested her head against his chest and he held her as she cried.

"You are what's important right now. And it's going to be all right."

"I can't stay here forever." She sniffed. "Shay has school." Her body shook. "I just can't go back there, Jack. I can't." She buried her face in his shirt. "What am I going to do?" She snorted a derisive chuckle. "At least I don't have to worry about a job." She sniffed hard and swiped at her wet eyes. "Travis made sure *his* wife didn't have to work. Biggest mistake I made other than marrying him was not holding on to some part of my identity." Her chest heaved. "I was just Travis Holder's wife and Shay's mommy." She cried harder.

"Shh. It's going to be okay. You are a helluva lot more than that bastard's wife and Shay's mother. You're my sister. That's what matters," he said in a teasing tone hoping to get her to smile.

She glanced up through tear-filled eyes and a smile crept across her mouth. She playfully socked him in the arm. "See what I mean? There's no me."

"There's plenty of you," he said seriously. "Look, we have the weekend to come up with a plan. On Monday, you're going to call Shay's school and tell them that there was a family emergency and she will be out for a few days. We'll take it from there. One day at a time."

Michelle sighed heavily and rested against her brother. "All right," she whispered.

Jackson leaned his head against the back of the couch and momentarily closed his eyes. This has been a day for the record books, he thought as he gently rocked his sister in his arms. First it was Victoria's cryptic bombshell, then Michelle showing up with her horrible news and then meeting Zoe Beaumont. It was almost too much to process. But he had to.

He didn't know who had it in for him at the college or why. Travis had an ass-whipping coming and Carla… Well, like his grandmother always said, God don't like ugly. Her day was sure to come. He gritted his teeth. Then there was Zoe. In the midst of all the turmoil and confusion she was the calm, the peace amid the storm. When he was with her, even for that short period of time, his mind and his spirit were at rest, as if he'd come home after a long journey. He didn't know how it was possible to feel that strongly about someone that you barely knew. But he *did* know her. A part of him knew her. He had no idea how or why, just that it was a truth that he accepted without question. Did Zoe feel the same connection?

"Wait, wait, tell me again," Sharlene squealed with excitement. "You find this little girl and it's his niece? O-M-G." She shook her head in amazement. "You know this is fate, girl, no two ways about it. And you can kick all that logic crap of yours out of the window, 'cause there is no explaining this."

Zoe hugged herself and scooted to the corner of the couch. "I'm really finding it hard to stick to my guns. I mean it's all so surreal." She reached for her glass of iced tea from the coffee table. "But what if it is true, that someone, some cosmic force or family legacy really brought us together. And what if we fall for each other and what if it doesn't work out, just like all the others? What then?"

"Zee, you can't think like that. Remember what Nana said. You're *the one,* girl, but you have to believe."

Zoe closed her eyes for a minute. She didn't know what to believe. The struggle in her mind still raged—logic versus the inexplicable. She had to admit that the instant she'd laid eyes on Jackson Treme, a trip wire went off inside her. There was a connection, a vibe, a sense of awareness that she had no way of explaining. And if she were to totally buy into the family lore, and what was expected of her, she could believe that he was *the one* who'd been sent to her. On the other hand it could be something as simple as good, old-fashioned lust.

Sharlene sipped her drink then put it down on the table. She leaned forward. "Tell me the story again."

"Sharl…" Zoe shook her head and smiled. "How many times have you heard the legend?"

"It doesn't matter," she said with a grin. "Come on. It's girl's night. If we were guys we'd been telling ghost stories or fish tales or trying to one-up each other's bedpost notches."

They both burst out laughing.

"All right, all right."

Sharlene settled back. She'd been hearing bits and pieces of the Beaumont legacy since she was a little girl. On more occasions than she could count, she would sit at the Beaumont kitchen table listening to Aunt Fern or Aunt Flo tell stories about their many loves, failed marriages and the reasons why. Or she'd become enthralled by Zoe's fabulous mother when she dressed up in all her fancy clothes to sing at a nightclub or hurry out to a waiting car that took her who knows where for months on end. But she never grew tired of the stories, the magic and mystery of it all.

"My great-great grandmother and grandfather were captured during a raid on their village in the ancient city of Djenne in Mali, West Africa," Zoe began in that sultry storytelling voice that Sharlene loved. "My great-great grandmother, Zinzi, was the conjure woman of the village. Everyone came to her with their problems. After she and my great-great-grandfather were taken and enslaved, the village slowly died off." She drew in a breath. "At least that's what Nana said. The village was wiped out. When they were brought to Louisiana, they were separated and sold off at auction. Nana said Zinzi's wails could be heard up and down the Mississippi. She was sold to Ezekiel Beaumont and she never saw her husband, Etu, again. The way the story goes, Ezekiel became so consumed by Zinzi that he put her up to live in his house, with his wife.

He even bought her freedom. Zinzi had three children by him—all girls. Nana said that Zinzi put a spell on him. And when he died, he didn't leave his wife a thing. He left it all to Zinzi and her daughters—the land, the house, all his money and even the servants who still remained after the Civil War.

"She was a wealthy woman. But she never got over losing Etu. She still cried for him and some nights she could be seen at the top of the hill just wandering around looking for her husband. One morning, her oldest daughter, Willa, found her up on the hill, slumped against the tree. She had a piece of cloth clutched in her hand. She'd often told her daughters it was the only thing she had left of her husband."

Zoe drew in a long breath and gave her head a quick shake, coming back to the here and now. She turned her faraway gaze toward Sharlene, who was entranced.

"So sad and beautiful," Sharlene murmured.

"Hmm. And every Beaumont woman since then has had nothing but heartache. All of their loves end in tragedy."

"It's like you all are being punished over and over again. But why? I never understood that."

"Neither did I until Nana told me on my last visit."

Sharlene leaned forward. "Well…what is it?"

"Zinzi and Etu's marriage was a sacred one. Their marriage brought together two of the most important tribes in Mali with all their riches and their powers. When they were taken from the village, what had been joined spiritually was broken. And until they found each other and were reunited as man and wife, happiness would remain elusive in their household. Zinzi and Etu never found each other."

"And heartache has continued to follow your family."

Zoe nodded. "Now you tell me that isn't a hard story to believe. I mean, I can totally understand being taken from Africa and sold into slavery, but curses and legacy and sacred bonds? And I'm supposed to somehow fix it all when no one before me could?" She shook her head.

"Did Nana tell you how?" Sharl cautiously asked.

Zoe looked right into the eyes of her best friend. Slowly she nodded. "Yes, she did."

Chapter 10

Jackson peeked in on Michelle and Shay. They were still sound asleep. He eased the door closed and went back downstairs. Even with all that had gone on, last night was the first night in weeks that he'd actually slept. He felt rested and ready to take on whatever came his way.

He went into the kitchen and made a pot of coffee then went out front and retrieved the newspaper. He snapped the paper open and walked back inside. The headlines featured the usual stories of unrest around the world, local and national politics. He turned to the Arts section and there smiling back at him was a photo of Zoe along with an interview she'd given about the opening. He sat down at the table and read the article but his gaze kept shifting back to her picture.

At the end of the article it gave the days and hours that the museum was open and how long the exhibit would be on display. He set the paper down and went to pour a mug of coffee. The schedule noted that the museum opened at noon on Saturday. He wondered if she was working today. He checked his watch. It was nearly ten-thirty. He listened for any movement upstairs. They were still asleep.

Getting up from the table he found some paper and a pen from the kitchen drawer and scribbled a quick note to his sister and posted it on the fridge. He scooped up his car keys from the table near the front door and headed out.

Zoe did a slow walk through the main hall of the museum, taking notes along the way and continued checking to make sure that nothing was broken or out of place. Although maintenance had already been through the entire space, she always felt better when she followed up. The museum was scheduled to open in another hour and although she didn't anticipate the crowd to be the size of the night before, Saturday was always busy.

She stopped just outside of the room that had been set aside for the exhibit. The statues sat regally on a pedestal. Slowly she approached. The closer she drew, the warmer she became as if the statues were radiating some kind of heat. She stopped in front of them.

"Do you really have some kind of power?" she asked cautiously. She laughed to herself. "Someone has to believe it, I suppose." She turned to leave and spotted Linda walking down the corridor.

"Linda."

She slowed and turned. "Oh, hi."

"I thought you were coming in at two."

She shrugged. "Figured I'd come in early and get some work out of the way."

Zoe walked toward her. "You okay?" she asked, referring to Linda's confession about her feelings for Mike the previous day.

Linda drew in a breath and slowly let it go. She forced a tight smile. "Yeah, I'm good. And I'm sorry about all that. No reason for me to lay my problems on you. It was totally out of character and I apologize."

"No need, really. I just want to make sure you're okay. I know it can't be easy feeling the way you do and working with Mike every day."

"It's not. But I'll figure it out."

"Have you ever had a real conversation with Mike?"

"What do you mean?"

"I mean a conversation that wasn't an argument. You're a wonderful woman. You're smart, your pretty, hardworking, independent. But to be honest, you don't let Mike see that."

Linda frowned in confusion. "I don't know what you mean. We work together practically every day."

"Yes, and because he doesn't see you the way you want him to, your frustrations come out. That's when tensions flare up between you two." She paused. "Listen, it's not my business, but I will give you this one piece of advice and then I'm going to leave it alone. Take it easy. Give yourself some breathing room and just be you. And if he can't see it, well, then maybe he's not the one."

Linda pursed her lips, and then slowly the corner of her mouth lifted ever so slightly. "Thanks," she said sincerely.

"Sure."

"I better get finished. I need to put out more brochures on each of the floors before we open."

Zoe nodded and watched her walk away before returning to her office. Imagine her giving advice on relationships when she hadn't had a serious one in longer than she cared to admit. But for some reason she felt infused with wisdom. She laughed and opened the door.

Before she had a chance to sit down, her phone rang. She rounded the desk and picked up the phone.

"Ms. Beaumont, speaking."

"There's a gentleman here to see you," the security guard said.

"Who is it?"

She heard some muffled conversation.

"Jackson Treme."

Zoe's heart jumped. "Um, let him know I'll be there in a moment." Her hand shook ever so slightly as she hung up the phone. She drew in a steadying breath, stood and tugged on the hem of her suit jacket. He was here. For an instant she squeezed her eyes shut then walked out to the main floor.

Jackson paced back and forth in front of the security desk. He'd rehearsed what he wanted to say on the drive over and all his thoughts had gone out of his head when he saw her coming his way.

"Mr. Treme." Did she sound as breathless as he felt?

"I'm sure you're busy—"

"No, not at all. I'm glad you came."

Jackson's dark eyes darkened even more and the warmth of his smile lit up her soul.

He took a step closer. The soft scent of her embraced him. "I'd like to come back when you get off. Take you out to dinner or a drink, whatever you want."

"I'm off at six."

"I'll be here waiting. Did you drive?"

"I actually walked today," she said.

Her eyes glided over his face. Her mouth was suddenly dry and when she ran her tongue across her lips, Jackson's body reacted instantly. Inadvertently he groaned deep in this throat.

Zoe reached for his arm. "Are you okay?"

"Yeah, yeah, fine." He swallowed. "Um, listen,

I'd better let you get back to work." He tugged in a breath. "I'll see you at six."

Zoe nodded and Jackson walked out.

On legs that suddenly felt weak and wobbly, she crossed the expansive floor, hurried back to her office and locked the door behind her. She flopped down in her chair, leaned back and spun around. When she came to a stop she shook her head in disbelief. She felt giddy as if she'd just been asked to the senior prom by the high-school heartthrob.

It was crazy the way she reacted to this man. She'd even agreed to a date without a second thought. "Crazy, just crazy," she said aloud.

She'd been out with her share of men. But she'd never allowed herself to let go, give in to her feelings. Part of that was because of what she'd seen happen to the women in her family, what she'd grown up with. And partly because there had never been anyone who made her feel anything beyond the superficial. Yet, Jackson Treme had been able to do that from the moment he'd grabbed her to keep her from falling. But hadn't all the other men who'd come into the Beaumont women's lives done the same thing? Look how that turned out.

She rested her arms on her desk then covered her face with her hands. What if Nana was wrong? What if all the dreams were just that, wishful fantasies with no substance? She wanted to just let go and give in to this glorious new feeling that Jackson had awakened in her, but she was so afraid.

Zoe looked at her watch. The museum was open now. She'd been there since ten o'clock, and she'd taken care of what she'd needed to. She picked up the phone and dialed Sharlene's cell phone. Sharl picked up on the third ring.

"Hey, sis. What's up?"

"I got a date."

"Get out! Wait, with Jackson?"

"Yes," she gushed.

Sharlene squealed her delight on the other end. "How or when did all this happen?"

Zoe gave her all the details.

"Well, I'll be. Now that's what I'm talking about—a man who takes charge. I like him already. So where are you two going?"

"I have no idea. But I thought if you had some time, we could go shopping. He's picking me up here at work and I have on a boring navy business suit."

"You don't have to ask me twice. You want to meet me here? We can go to Vintage on Market. I love that place."

"You know better than I do. I'm heading over there as we speak. I should be there in about fifteen minutes."

"See you in a few." She disconnected the call, pulled open the bottom drawer of her desk, took out her purse and walked out.

Her step felt light as she walked along Peachtree Street. The weather was exquisite. There wasn't a cloud in the sky. She pulled in a long lungful of spring air and lifted her face toward the warmth of the sun.

She turned the corner onto the street where Sharlene's shop was located and stopped dead in her tracks. She peered a bit closer certain that she was seeing things. But she wasn't. Seated on a bench under a tree on the opposite side of the street, eating what looked like her favorite Pinkberry yogurt was Mike and Linda. They were deep in conversation and apparently oblivious to anyone or anything.

"Well, I'll be." She smiled to herself. Maybe her words of wisdom to Linda made some sense after all. Obviously something had happened. She'd love to be a fly on the bench and eavesdrop on their conversation.

Picking up her pace she continued down the street until she reached Moore Designs. Wait until she told Sharlene. Maybe it's the weather, she thought.

"You have got to be kidding," Sharlene said as they walked out. She kept peeking over her shoulder hoping to spot the new couple.

Zoe nudged her in the arm. "Would you stop? You'd make the worst spy."

"You have to admit it's hard to imagine if you don't see it with your own eyes. Mike actually grinds his teeth when he talks about Linda."

Zoe laughed. "Oh, stop. He does not. Well, maybe sometimes."

"See?" Sharlene chuckled. "Vintage is right around the corner. Come on." She hooked her arm through Zoe's.

For the next hour they combed the racks and tables, searching for the perfect outfit.

"I don't want anything too suggestive," Zoe said, when Sharlene held up a sleeveless black number with a nice split up the left side. "And not black. I mean, it's an after-work dinner. It's too much."

Sharlene flashed her a "you have got to be kidding me" look. "A little black dress is always appropriate," she said drily. She pushed aside a few more dresses on the rack and finally pulled out a soft, Wedgewood blue dress in a bamboo cotton and spandex mix. It had an utterly feminine rosette detail, a draped waistline and a slimming sash with a hemline that just kissed the knee. The deep neckline was tempting, but tasteful. She held it up. "This is perfect for you. With those size C-cups and those legs, you'll be a knockout."

Zoe reached for the dress and loved it on sight. "What size it is?" She lifted the tag. "Ten." She looked at Sharlene with beginnings of a smile on her lips. "Just my size." She checked the price tag and her mouth dropped open. "A hundred and fifty dollars! Sharlene!" She shoved the dress back at her. "I'm not paying that much money for a dress that I'll probably never wear again, or worse, feel like

I have to wear all the time to compensate for the money I spent on it."

"Oh, stop! Splurge a little. When was the last time you did something for yourself—something spontaneous and completely out of character? Here, just feel it. Imagine the feel of it against your skin. Imagine Jackson when he sees you in it." She winked and shook the dress in front of Zoe in a teasing fashion.

Zoe made a face and finally snatched the dress. "Okay, you win." She hugged the dress to her. "I don't have anything to go with this."

"Easily fixed, my sister," she said and steered her toward accessories.

By the time they walked out nearly an hour and a half later, Zoe's credit card was two hundred and fifty dollars heavier.

"So have you thought any more about the offer to go to New York?" Sharlene asked as they walked back.

"No. Not really. So much has happened so quickly. I'm not sure what I'm going to do."

"It's a fantastic opportunity for you and it would be a serious boost to your career."

Zoe nodded in agreement.

"I hear a but."

Zoe threw her a look. "I have to see how things go."

"Between you and Jackson?"

"Yes."

Sharlene smiled to herself. Maybe Zoe was beginning to believe after all.

They stopped in front of Sharlene's office. "Call me the minute you get home and let me know how it went."

"I promise."

"And just relax and have fun, if for no other reason than because you deserve it. You haven't been out on a real date in ages. You're long overdue."

"All right, all right. Don't rub it in," she joked. She kissed her friend's cheek. "I'll call you."

She started off down the block in the direction of the museum. The next four hours were the longest of her life.

Chapter 11

Jackson stirred the pot of chili. He sprinkled more cayenne pepper and lowered the flame. Since he would be eating out, he'd prepared his favorite recipe for his sister and niece. He was really worried about Michelle. Travis's betrayal was hitting her hard. One minute she seemed like she was holding it together and the next she was in a daze. Other times he would walk into a room and find her crying.

He couldn't begin to imagine the kind of pain that she felt. Even though he and Carla had broken up a while back, he was devastated and sickened by what she'd done to his sister—his sister of all people. Michelle had befriended her. They'd hung out together, traveled in some of the same circles.

It was unthinkable. Yet he couldn't decide who was worst, Travis or Carla. How long had it been going on? Were they seeing each other when he was still seeing Carla? What kind of people had he and his sister fallen for?

He put a pot of water on to boil, added a dash of salt and some olive oil for the rice.

When he and Michelle were growing up, their parents used to fix chili and rice on Saturdays. It was always a treat. They were each assigned a task in preparing the meal: adding the ingredients, grating the cheese, steaming the beans, browning the meat or fixing the rice. He still carried on the tradition. And at least one Saturday a month he fixed chili just the way his family had when he was a kid. He hoped it would stir up some pleasant memories for Michelle, at least for a little while.

"Is that the famous Treme chili I smell?" Michelle yawned as she walked into the kitchen. She came up behind Jackson and wrapped her arms around his waist.

"The nose knows." He poured in two cup of rice and covered the pot.

"Remember those Saturdays?"

"Absolutely. I figured it would be like the old times, a pleasant memory." He turned around.

Michelle looked up into his eyes that were identical to her own. "I could use that right now." She backed away and lowered her head.

Jackson lifted her chin with the tip of his finger.

"I don't like tears in my chili," he teased. "And I was thinking that maybe it's time we carried on the tradition. Share the famous family recipe with Shay."

Michelle wiped away a sniffle and a slow smile gently blossomed. "I think she'd like that."

"Great. You remember all the ingredients, right?"

"Of course!" she said.

He wiped his hands on a dishtowel. "Good. I got the basics started and you can finish up with Shay while I get ready for a date."

"A date! With…with Zoe?"

He grinned like he'd won the lottery. "Yep. I'm picking her up at six."

Michelle leaped up and wrapped her arms around his neck. "I am sooo crazy happy for you." She kissed him all over his face. "How did all this happen?"

"If you let go of my neck I swear I'll tell you," he said, chuckling.

She settled down and sat in a chair. She crossed her legs and waited. Jackson leaned against the fridge and told her about going to the museum and asking for her.

"So you just asked her out to dinner and she said yes? You could be a serial killer," she said with a grin.

"Thanks, sis."

"You know what I mean. You don't know each other."

"Last time I checked that's how people *got* to know each other. Dinner, lunch, talking." He winked.

"I guess it's been a while," she said softly and lowered her gaze.

Jackson came over to her. He took her hand. "Hey, sorry."

"It's all right." She stroked his cheek. "I'm happy for you. I really am."

"Thanks." He kissed the tip of her nose. "So I'm going to leave Shay and the Treme family recipe in your very capable hands. I don't want to be late." He started out of the kitchen.

"She's a lucky lady, Jack."

Jackson glanced back over his shoulder. "I have a feeling that I'm the lucky one."

Zoe was a bundle of nerves as six o'clock approached. She'd changed clothes an hour earlier and spent the rest of the time pacing back and forth in her office. She'd called Sharlene at least three different times just to be reminded that she was going to have a wonderful time.

She'd been so consumed with her impending date that she'd totally forgotten about seeing Mike and Linda together earlier in the afternoon until Linda knocked on her office door.

"Come in."

Linda eased the door open and stuck her head

in. Her eyes widened in surprise when she saw Zoe all dressed up.

"Wow. Is it okay if I come in?"

Zoe's face heated. "Sure."

Linda came in and closed the door behind her. "Great dress."

"Thanks." She quickly sat down and tried to look busy as she began flipping through papers on her desk. "What can I do for you?"

"You already did it."

Zoe looked up. "What do you mean?"

"I talked to Mike today, like you said."

Zoe folded her nervous fingers together. The scene she'd witnessed earlier played in her mind's eye. "What happened?"

"He listened. I told him that I realized that I was making his life miserable, but it wasn't my intention. I told him that sometimes I have an unorthodox way of letting someone know that I'm…interested in them."

Zoe smiled. "And?"

"He said he thought I hated his guts. That's why he never asked me out before."

"What?" Her expression brightened with delight. "So did he ask you out?"

Linda bobbed her head. "We're going to Gladys Knight's place tonight. Can you believe it?"

Zoe laughed. "Yes, I think I do." *Amazing things just kept happening.* "I'm glad for you, Linda. I really am."

"Thanks. And, uh, I really appreciate the advice. I was making a mess of things." She paused. "You look like you have a date yourself."

Zoe cleared her throat. "I do. Well, not exactly. Yes, I do."

"Well, whichever it is, have a good time." She backed up toward the door.

"You, too."

"Thanks. Good night." She opened the door and walked out.

Must be the weather. She took a quick look at her watch. It was five minutes to six. Her heart started racing. She tapped her fingers on the desk. She didn't want to keep him waiting, but she didn't want to appear overeager and be downstairs waiting before he arrived. Maybe he was going to be late. But if he was going to be late, he would have called. Then again maybe he wouldn't. Maybe he was the kind of guy who didn't care about making others wait for them. Maybe he... She jumped at the sound of her phone ringing. She looked at the flashing extension number. It was security.

She snatched up the phone. "Ms. Beaumont."

"Yes, there's a Mr. Treme here to see you. I told him we were closed."

"I'll be right there, Frank. Thank you." She hung up the phone. "Oh, my goodness." *He was really here.*

She pushed back from her seat and all of a sudden her mind went blank. Where was her purse? Her keys? Should she take the shawl that Sharlene insisted she buy? What if she was overdressed? He never said where they were going. "Get a grip," she said out loud. She drew in a deep breath, opened the bottom drawer of her desk and took out her purse where she always kept it. She opened it and her keys were inside as they always were. She took the shawl that was draped across the back of the chair and put it over her arm. She took one last look around her office, turned off the light and walked out.

Jackson wasn't sure what to expect, but the vision that was coming toward him was more than he could have ever imagined. She was stunning. The blue against her bronze skin was mouthwatering. She'd styled her hair in an updo. The combination of the hairstyle and the deep neckline of her dress nearly did him in. He was staring so hard that it took him a moment to realize that she'd stopped walking and was standing right in front of him.

"Sorry if I kept you waiting," she said.

Jackson swallowed the tightness in his throat that matched the one in his groin. "I'd wait all night if that's what it would take to see you. You look incredible."

She started to say something silly like "this old thing," but good sense intervened. "Thank you."

"Ready?"

She didn't trust her voice when he was looking

at her like that, as if he could see into her soul. She nodded her head instead.

"I'm parked right out front."

"Good night, Frank," she managed.

"You two have a nice time."

Jackson looked back. "Thanks."

"I hope you like soul food," Jackson said as he opened the car door and helped her in.

She turned to look at him and their gazes collided. Heat stirred her body. "What self-respecting Southern girl doesn't like soul food?" she said with laughter in her voice.

"A woman after my own heart." He shut the door and hurried around to the driver's side. He stuck the key in the ignition and Marvin Gaye's classic, "Let's Get it On," filled the interior. They both burst out laughing and the tension evaporated like morning mist.

"I swear I didn't plan that," he said as he slowly pulled off.

"That's what they all say," she said.

He gave her a quick look. "I would think that would be something you wouldn't know anything about."

"Really. And why would you think that?"

"Because I think that you are the kind of woman who can sense a line a mile away. And the poor fool who tried to hand you one would never get the chance."

"Is that right?" She relaxed against the soft

leather interior and angled her body in his direction. "And what else have you surmised about me in the less than twenty-four hours that we've known each other?"

"That you think about things before you do them. You look at all the possibilities. You don't like mistakes or having regrets."

Her brows rose. "And you know all of this how?"

He came to a stop at a red light and turned fully toward her. He looked directly into her eyes. "I don't know. I just do."

Zoe felt as if the air had been sucked from her lungs. As illogical as all this was, it made perfect sense.

Chapter 12

The streets of Atlanta were teeming with Saturday night diners and partygoers. Rather than spend half of their evening hunting for a parking space, Jackson parked in a nearby municipal garage and they walked the two blocks back to the restaurant.

"I love Mary Mac's Tea Room," Zoe cried when she realized where they were going. "I haven't been here since I first moved to Atlanta."

"This will be my first time. I heard it was great." He opened the door for her. "I made reservations for the Skyline Room. They have a piano player tonight."

"Can't wait."

"Good evening and welcome to Mary Mac's.

Do you have reservations?" the hostess asked from behind the podium.

"Yes, two for Treme." He placed his hand at the small of Zoe's back.

Zoe felt her insides quiver. The heat of his hand scorched her skin. She drew in a sharp breath and concentrated on putting one foot in front of the other as they were led to their table.

After the waitress seated them she ran through the house specials then took their drink orders. Zoe ordered an apple martini. Jackson opted for Rob Roy on the rocks.

"When we walked up, you said you came here when you first moved to Atlanta." He tilted his head to the side. "Where did you live before you moved here?"

"New Orleans. Born and raised."

Jackson's skin tingled. "New Orleans?"

"Mmm-hmm." She opened the menu.

"So was I."

Zoe's gaze lifted. "What?"

"I grew up in New Orleans. I only moved to Atlanta a little more than a year ago."

Zoe blinked back her surprise. "And we had to move all the way to Atlanta to meet each other. How crazy is that?"

"No crazier than anything else that's happened since we met." He leaned forward. "I don't know if you feel it, but ever since that day of the fire when

I saw you for the first time, it felt like it wasn't the first time. I mean…"

"I know exactly what you mean," she said, with a lilt of surprise in her voice.

His eyes creased at the corners, studying her face seeing if he could discover the truth there. Was she simply humoring him or did she really believe what she'd said?

"It's been like that for me, too." She swallowed. "I can't explain it." After the words were out of her mouth she couldn't believe she'd said them to a man she barely knew. *But you do know him. He's always been there. Waiting for you.* It was her grandmother's voice in her head as clear as if she were sitting right beside her.

Jackson's mouth lifted in a slow smile. His eyes moved leisurely over her face before reaching across the table to take her hand. He ran his thumb over the smooth surface of her knuckles sending tremors scurrying up her arm.

The waitress returned with their drinks, but the connection between them wasn't broken. They barely noticed her and absentmindedly ordered the house special.

"Where did you grow up?" Jackson asked.

"On Montiere," she said, her Creole accent creeping in. "The big white house on the corner."

He tossed his head back and laughed. "I used to ride by there on my bike as a kid. Always wondered who lived in that big old house."

"That was us. The Beaumonts. House was handed down from one generation to the next."

"Who lives there now?"

"My mother, and her sisters and my grandmother. All women all the time," she said with a light laugh.

He rested his arms on the table. "Tell me about your family."

"What do you want to know?"

"Whatever you want to tell me."

"Why don't you go first?" she challenged.

He reached for his glass and took a short swallow. "Okay. Let's see. I have a twin sister. Her name is Michelle and I have an older brother, Franklin. We lost our parents about eight years ago…one after the other."

"I'm sorry."

"You met my niece, Shay. Basically, we're your average family. My parents worked hard. My dad worked for the railroad. My mother was a teacher."

"You took after her."

"Yeah, I think I did."

"Did you always like art?"

"For as long as I can remember. I thought I would be an artist, but I'm really not that good. Michelle was the one who convinced me to get my degree and teach."

"Why did you leave New Orleans?"

He glanced away for a minute. So far the conversation had been pretty normal, the kind most couples have on first dates. If he told her the real reason why he'd broken up with his fiancé, left all his friends and family behind because of a feeling he had and dreams he'd dreamed, she just might get up and walk out.

"Let's just say that I didn't think I could find what I was searching for back home." He roamed her face with his eyes.

"What *are* you looking for?" she asked, holding her breath in anticipation.

"My future."

The moment gently held them.

"Do you think you'll find your future here?" she asked, barely above a whisper.

"It's beginning to look that way. What about you? Why did you leave the Big Easy?"

She chuckled a little. "To get away from the burden of family expectations."

"Hmm. Family is usually the hardest on you." He slowly turned his glass on the table. "What did they want you to do that you were dead set against?"

Fulfill their lives, fix the past, be responsible for things that she wasn't a part of. But saying that would make her sound selfish. She wasn't. She loved her family. But what they wanted from her, what they expected from her frightened her.

"Oh, the usual," she said, blowing it off. "Settle down, marry and have a bunch of kids."

"I would think you could manage that with your eyes closed and your hands tied behind you."

She shrugged slightly. "I wanted my own life,

to live my own dreams. Not someone else's," she added, the passion of her conviction strengthening her voice.

"Have you?"

"I'm still working on it," she conceded. "But I believe I'm moving in the right direction."

The waitress returned with their dinner and they spent the next half hour savoring the delicious food in between sharing some of their favorite recipes.

"No one can make peach cobbler like my Nana Zora."

Jackson wagged his fork at her. "Hands down I make the best chili this side of the Mississippi bar none."

"Really?" She cocked her head to the side. "I'd take bets on that one, mister."

"Say what. You?"

"Yes. You better believe it."

"Sounds like a showdown to me."

"Whenever you get up the nerve."

"Ohhh." He slapped his palm against his chest, and chuckled hard. "It's like that?"

"All week including Sundays," she tossed back loving the banter.

He leaned forward. "I'm ready when you are. You name the time and place and I'm there."

She curved her mouth to the side and narrowed her gaze. "Hmm. Two weeks from Sunday. My place. Noon."

"Don't be late."

Zoe cracked up.

The waitress came and cleared away the plates and offered a dessert menu.

"I'm fine, thanks," Zoe said and handed the menu back.

"Nothing for me, either. You can bring the bill, thanks." He leaned back in his seat totally relaxed, totally captivated by Zoe and he didn't want the night to end. "It's still early. You want to do something? Maybe go listen to some jazz? Take a walk, see a movie?"

"Hmm. It is early. I wouldn't mind taking a walk."

"A walk it is."

The waitress returned with the bill and Jackson handed over his credit card.

"I'm going to the restroom," Zoe said, getting up from her seat.

Jackson jumped up and pulled out her chair. As he reached around her she turned and found herself in his arms, the swell of her breasts pressed against the wall of his chest.

Zoe's breath caught and she fell into the depths of his eyes, which seemed to engulf her. She inhaled the totally male scent of him that went straight to her head, jumbling her thoughts and for a moment she'd forgotten why she'd gotten up or where she was going.

"I'll wait for you up front," he said, his voice thick and low.

She wet her lips with a slow dance of her tongue. "Be right back," she managed. She stepped around him and her thigh brushed against the rise of his erection. A tremor shot through her and piqued the tiny bud between her thighs. She heard the almost imperceptible groan rumble deep in his throat as he sucked in air through his teeth. Or maybe it was her moan that she heard and silently prayed that she wouldn't do something silly—like trip over her feet before she could get behind closed doors and pull herself together.

Once inside the ladies room she dared to breathe. Her heart pounded and she felt flushed. "God." Her eyelids fluttered as she relived the feel of him against her. Just for an instant and her entire mind was in a knot. She stared at herself in the mirror, certain that she was going to see a new face, a new person. But she didn't. Yet it was her and not her at the same time. She looked the same on the outside but inside she felt different, as if a switch had been turned on and her body was charged with electricity.

Her hand shook as she took her lipstick out of her purse and reapplied the soft coral color. "I hope you're right, Nana," she said to her reflection. "Because I think I might be willing to open my heart this time." She dropped her lipstick into her purse and headed back out.

Chapter 13

The heavens were a dusty dark blue, cloudless, with pinpoints of light as the stars illuminated the canvas of night. Jazz, hip-hop and R&B could be heard as doors to cafes and nightclubs opened and closed to a rhythm that was unique to a Saturday night in Atlanta.

They walked in companionable silence, taking in the sights and sounds with no particular destination in mind, when Zoe spotted a Pinkberry.

"Oh, we've got to stop."

"Stop where?"

"At Pinkberry. They have absolutely, hands down, the best frozen yogurt on the planet."

Jackson laughed. "All that, huh. Guess I should try some."

"You have to," she said as if not doing so was the most outlandish thing she'd heard. Without thinking, she grabbed his hand and pulled him behind her through the glass door.

"Mango is my favorite," she said as she pretended to whisper. "But any of them are good."

They inched along the line.

Jackson watched in amusement as her face lit up as she talked about something as simple as frozen yogurt, and relished the fact that she still held his hand.

Her soft fingers felt good in his. He wanted to hold her tighter, but didn't want to break the spell. To him it felt like the most natural thing in the world.

She turned to gaze up and him, the most delightful smile on her face.

"Do you know what you want?"

That was a loaded question, he thought. "Um, I'll have what you're having."

Zoe stepped up to the counter and ordered two medium mango yogurts to go.

Reluctantly, Jackson released her hand, took out his wallet and paid for their desserts.

"We can sit over there," Jackson said, lifting his chin toward a bank of tables and benches in the pedestrian plaza.

"Sure."

They stepped off the curb and onto the island that was cut off from traffic for one block and adorned with benches, tables and chairs in between potted trees and shrubbery.

Jackson spotted a curved bench with a round table and they walked over. Zoe scooted onto the bench and Jackson slid over beside her.

"I can never get over how crowded it is at night," Jackson said, before taking his first taste of the yogurt. "Hmm."

"Told ya." Zoe beamed. She put a spoonful in her mouth and closed her eyes as the pleasure trickled through her. "My one guilty pleasure."

"Just one?"

She looked across at him from under her long lashes. "So far."

"How about if I said something crazy like, let me be another one of your guilty pleasures?"

Her cheeks heated. She slowly licked the confection from her spoon. "And what if I said I think I'd like that very much." She held her breath.

Jackson draped his arm behind her. His fingers played with one of her curls that had come loose. His eyes moved slowly across her face, down the curve of her slender neck to the rise of her breasts before returning to her lips.

Zoe's lips parted in anticipation as he drew nearer until his image blurred and the tenderness of his mouth blended with hers. His fingers threaded along the back of her neck easing her closer and they shared the sticky mango sweetness as their mouths met and mingled, tasting and testing.

The urge to possess her completely rose inside him with such force that he had to tear himself away. But then her tongue teased the contours of his lips and any hope of freeing himself was gone. He could feel the blood pounding in his head, *and the sound of tribal drums filling the night air. He was running. He could feel them coming behind him. The sound of the hounds barking in the night. He knew that if he could make it to the river they would lose his scent and he would have a chance. He had to survive.*

Zoe's soft sighs interrupted the images that had enveloped him dragging him back to some unknown place. The drumming grew faint, the scent of the river faded and the hounds stopped their terrifying howling.

Shaken, Jackson eased back. The expression in Zoe's eyes let him know that she had been there, too.

"Zoe." He whispered her name like a prayer. "I don't know what just happened." He ran his finger along the soft curve of her jaw. She shuddered at his touch.

"Neither do I," she said, as her breathing kicked up a notch. "I… I wasn't here. I mean I was here physically, but…"

"I know," he said urgently. "That's the same way I felt. Like an out-of-body experience."

She wanted to tell him what was happening to her, the dreams and the burden that weighed on her mind. She needed to share it with him and only him. But she was afraid. *Just be yourself,* she heard herself saying to Linda, and recalled the image of Linda and Mike earlier. That moment had been a turning point for them. And here she was at that same crossroads. She shifted her gaze away. "Wow, the yogurt is melting."

"We can get some more if you want."

"No. I'm fine. I am getting a little tired though."

Jackson stood. "I better get you home then."

They walked back toward the garage and this time it was Jackson who reached for Zoe's hand. They strolled together slowly, talking and laughing softly about the music that they liked growing up, the troubles that the Gulf Coast had experienced after Katrina and their passion for African art.

"I've been collecting pieces for years," Zoe said as Jackson slowed the car when he pulled onto her street.

"Really?"

"From all parts of Africa, particularly Mali. It's where my ancestors are from."

"You traced your ancestry?"

"Since I was a little girl, my family has always talked about where our family came from. According to Nana Zora and the stories that she was told by her mother and grandmother, great-great-grandmother Zinzi was a conjure woman and head of her village. She was married to Etu, the son of the chief of the adjoining village…" She told him about their capture and how they were separated when they were brought to Louisiana and sold at auction. She left out the part about the legacy and the heartache that has haunted her family for generations. Perhaps the time would come later.

"The house and the land that we lived on was the house of the former slave owner, Ezekiel Beaumont."

"Amazing," he said.

"My house is the one on the right."

Jackson eased to a stop in front of her house and cut off the engine. He turned to her. "Home safe and sound."

She lowered her head then looked directly at him. "I'm suddenly not so tired anymore." She hesitated a moment. "And I'm not ready for the night to end."

"Neither am I." He ran a finger across her brow.

"Would you like to come in for a little while? I think I have some wine and plenty of music."

"Sounds like a plan."

She drew in a breath, turned and unlocked her door.

"These pieces are incredible," he said admiring the small sculptures on the shelves and tabletops and the artwork on the white walls. "This is better than some galleries I've seen."

"Thank you." She handed him his glass of wine.

He raised his glass to hers. "To a wonderful evening and more to come."

Zoe touched her glass to his and took a tiny sip. "So what would you like to listen to?"

"Why don't you choose? I'm easy."

"Okay." She set down her glass and crossed the hardwood floors to a built-in wall cabinet. She opened the double doors in the center of the cabinet to reveal a fifty-two-inch television and a stereo system that could easily find its way into a recording studio. Inside were racks of CDs and albums. She slowly spun the rack and picked out six CDs and put them in the player. Moments later the sultry, plaintive voice of Billie Holiday filled the room with her signature song, "God Bless the Child."

"Aww, Billie," Jackson said. He put his glass down on an end table and turned toward Zoe. He held out his hand. "Dance with me."

Zoe's heart thundered in her chest and her legs felt weak as she placed her hand in his. Slowly he gathered her close until nothing but the fabric of their clothing separated them.

They swayed together in perfect harmony as if they'd always danced together. As Billie soothed them, Zoe felt her body relax and melt against Jackson. She closed her eyes and gave herself over to the moment.

As the song came to its pitch-perfect end, Jackson lifted Zoe's chin with the tip of his finger. They stood motionless, caught in each other's gaze.

Whatever hesitation she may have felt dissipated. She wanted him and she wanted him to want her just as much.

And he did.

The kiss was slow as he brushed his lips across hers. He teased her bottom lip with his teeth then his tongue, and delighted in feeling her body shiver against his. He cupped the back of her head in his large palm and drew her closer to him. Her lips parted ever so slightly and he teased them apart farther with his tongue until she let him in.

Her soft moan drifted into his soul and he felt like the sun had found a place inside him. She curled against him, igniting a full-blown erection that shook him to his core. His hands stroked her back, her arms, caressed her hips. He wanted to explore all of her if she'd let him.

Zoe eased down one strap of her dress and then the other. Jackson picked up the invitation and lowered the top of her dress to her waist to expose her full breasts.

His lips dropped from her mouth and skimmed her long neck, suckling the tender space near her collarbone. She whimpered and desire fueled his exploration. Her skin felt like silk and smelled like forever. If he lived to be one hundred he would never get enough of her scent. He planted hot kisses along the rise of her breasts.

She arched her back in offering, and he took the succulent fruit into his mouth, tasting and teasing the sweet brown nipples until she trembled, gripping his arms to keep from crumbling at his feet.

He was so hard that he hurt and he took her hand and placed it on his need, making her understand what she was doing to him and how much he wanted her.

Zoe's touch was like a branding iron, hot and steamy and a strangled groan rose from the bottom of his feet when she began a slow and deliberate massage, gripping and releasing him in a maddening rhythm.

The music swelled in the background as Billie released that last heart-wrenching note then segued to "Body and Soul."

Zoe took a small step back. She was on fire and she needed Jackson to douse the flames that threatened to consume her. "Come with me," she said in a husky voice. She took his hand and led him down the hallway to her bedroom. She opened the door and looked at him over her shoulder. Once she crossed the threshold there was no turning back. Yet she felt in her heart that making love to Jackson was so right.

She stepped inside and Jackson followed. She walked to her bed and sat down on the edge. Jackson slowly approached. He took her hands and pulled her to her feet.

"I want to see all of you." He slid her dress down over her hips so that it fell to the floor. She stepped over the pool that it made at her feet. She was bare except for a tiny black lace thong that she was so happy she'd decided to wear.

He reached out and touched her right breast. His palm grazed her hardened nipple. Her eyelids fluttered. He moved closer, lowered his head and took her into his mouth. She moaned in pleasure.

Zoe fumbled with the buttons of his shirt and wondered why her fingers wouldn't follow her commands. Finally she managed to get them opened and tugged his shirt off. Jackson tossed it to the floor. She went for his belt buckle, the rising desire and blinding need sabotaged her rational, conservative self. She wasn't thinking with her head. Her body was totally in charge. When she unzipped him and felt the hard weight of him in the palm of her hand she felt wet between her legs.

Jackson instinctively knew that she was flowing and readying herself for him. He looped one arm around her waist to hold her in place and his other slipped between her sweet thighs and fingered the swollen clit that longed for his attention.

"Ahhhh." She sucked in air. Her knees weakened.

Jackson eased her back onto the bed. He stepped out of his pants and shorts and joined her. They stretched out side-by-side facing each other. He kissed her softly on the mouth, down her neck, between the swell of her breasts, down the center of her body and played for a moment with her navel. Her skin quivered beneath his lips.

All the while his fingers explored her and her

body bathed them with her essence. Her pelvis moved instinctively in slow circles, while his fingers slid in and out and in and out.

Zoe gripped the sheets in her fists and pushed her heels into the mattress when he moved down between her trembling thighs. His mouth cupped her sex, sucked her in before dipping his tongue into the valley of honey.

Her entire body jerked. The muscles in her stomach fluttered. He grabbed her hips and licked and laved her until she was like butter, melting under his ministrations.

"Jackson!" she cried out tossing her head back and forth in the throes of passion.

"I'm right here, baby," he said. "Let it happen. Let me love you." He took her in his mouth again and the fire grew.

The flames began at her feet and traveled up her legs, raced along her body and ignited her breasts before exploding into an inferno that sent her screams of release soaring into the air in concert with Billie's "Me and My Man."

Jackson knew he couldn't hold out much longer but he wanted her to be totally satisfied. He wanted her to remember this first night the way he knew he would remember it—that it was the turning point in their lives, a coupling that would change them forever. He didn't know how he knew it he simply did, he thought as he moved between her legs.

He draped her legs over his arms and rose up on

his knees. His erection was so hard that it jumped and pulsed, took on a life of its own, tugging him toward satisfaction.

When his hot tip touched her wet opening, it took all of his willpower to keep from exploding.

Zoe wrapped her arms around his neck and pulled him to her. She tasted herself on his mouth and sucked on his bottom lip with her teeth.

Jackson pushed in just a little. The throbbing head crossed the moist threshold.

Zoe moaned, pressing her fingers into his back. She squeezed her eyes shut as he arched her legs higher and wider and entered her fully.

"Ohhhh," he groaned as her walls tightened and surrounded him.

The room moved into the distance. The music shifted from the bluesy tones of Billie to a pulsing drumbeat and bare feet dancing and pounding on dusty earth. Brilliant colors flashed in the distance as the tribesmen and women celebrated the consummation of Zinzi and Etu. The newly married couple moved together reaching a crescendo of celebration as they learned each other's bodies in the rhythm as old as time. The union was a sacred one, destined to be and all the more potent because of the true love that blazed in Zinzi's eyes as she lay beneath her husband, welcoming him into the dark hot valley of her body, crying out when he met the slightest resistance before breaking through the thin veil that separated them.

The pounding beat of the drums joined with the macaw cries of the women of the village and rushed through their veins intensifying the moment. Zinzi raised her legs higher, and opened for her husband. And the drums beat faster, louder carrying the newly joined couple along the rushing waters of the river, above the branches of the highest trees, tossing them against the heavens where they burst into a million pinpricks of light, becoming one with the stars above.

The images bloomed and the past and present merged, sucking Zoe and Jackson into the twisting, turning funnel of ecstasy that roared through Jackson gushing through Zoe's walls, to erupt in her soul sending her on a spiraling journey of unspeakable joy. Their strangled cries of release rose and met Billie's final note of "As Time Goes By."

Chapter 14

Jackson wrapped his arm around Zoe's waist and held her as close as their spooning bodies would allow. He buried his head in her hair and let the essence of her scent drift through and quiet the racing beat of his heart and the tumultuous thoughts that tore through his head.

He wasn't sure what had happened between them. He was here with her, inside of her but at the same time he felt as if he'd been transported someplace else in the distant past. That was crazy, of course, because he was right here in her bed in her house on Drew Lane in Atlanta, Georgia. Yet, it felt like a dream that had somehow come alive. He cupped her breast in his palm and tenderly kissed the back of her neck. This was no dream.

Zoe stared into the darkness, listening to the comforting beat of Jackson's heart against her back. She'd been there, on the mat in a small hut with the villagers drumming and dancing in celebration of the consummation of her marriage. But she wasn't married. She was a single woman, with a history of mediocre relationships, a family tree with leaves that shook, a job that she loved and a man in her bed who she'd only recently met but somehow had known forever. How could all of that be true at once? Zoe wondered if he'd had the same experience. The same waking dream that she'd had the instant he'd entered her. She shivered. Jackson pulled her closer.

"Something happened," he whispered into the night.

Zoe's senses heightened. "Something...?"

"I've never felt that way before. Been to that place." Jackson exhaled audibly. "I can't explain it." He kissed her shoulder and caressed her breast, teasing the nipple back to erection. He felt himself growing hard again.

Zoe moaned when her swollen clit twitched in response to his increasing caresses. She pressed her rear against his rising member and gyrated her hips until he thought he would go mad. She twisted her body away from him until she was facing him. She cupped his face and kissed him long and deep then pushed him onto his back before straddling him.

She felt free and totally uninhibited as she rose up then slowly lowered herself onto the length of him.

Jackson squeezed the taut globes of her rear and pulled her fully down onto him. Her head flung back and the veins in her neck stood out as she was totally impaled on the hard shaft that pulsed deep within her.

Zoe leaned forward and gripped the headboard to steady herself as she began a languid ride. Their bodies moved in perfect symmetry, flowing one onto the other, letting the sensations guide them, the intensity increase their speed.

The headboard banged steadily against the wall. The mattress gave and released as Jackson pushed upward, willing his body to touch the core of her. "Come on baby. Come to me," he ground out.

Zoe's heart pounded like crazy against her chest making her light-headed and her breath come in short gasps. "Right there, right there," she groaned, thrusting her pelvis forward and the muscles in her body tightened and that white hot heat sluiced through her veins, then pooled in the pit of her stomach. Her walls clenched and her entire body shook as the grip and release of her shuddering orgasm milked Jackson down to the bone.

When Zoe opened her eyes, the first light of daybreak lurked just beyond the horizon. Jackson stirred beside her. In the filtered daylight, she studied this man she'd lain with. In a word, he was beautiful. He was physically fit from head to toe, with toned muscles that rippled when he moved and a rock hard stomach that could easily be in a body-building infomercial. His skin was just rough enough to keep it from being soft, and his scent when she pressed her face to his flesh drove her crazy.

Tenderly her hand trailed the length of his side and across his flat belly, and moved lower to stroke his treasure. The air caught momentarily in her lungs as her fingers traversed the silky skin that covered his penis that even at half mast was long and thick.

She moaned softly, letting her fingers wrap around him. He was simply magnificent. She'd been with men before. She'd had great orgasms, but none had filled her. None had stretched her to her limits. None had made her see things, leave her body and come back for more. No, none of the others had done that. She stroked him now, slow and steady, reveling in her power to make him rise fully in her hand and hear his moans of pleasure as he awakened.

Zoe wanted to taste him, to feel the pulse of the veins in her mouth, run her tongue along the sleek head and make it weep. She licked the very tip then began making tiny circles until her lips captured him.

"Ahhhh." He laced his fingers through her hair

and sucked in air through clenched teeth, knowing that all he could do was give her what she'd wanted and enjoy the ride.

In the full light of day, Zoe expected to feel shy or awkward. Oddly enough, she didn't. Moving around in her kitchen preparing breakfast and listening to Jackson sing off-key in the shower seemed like the most natural thing in the world.

She poured orange juice into a glass carafe, scooped softly whipped eggs onto a platter alongside whole wheat French toast and fat turkey sausage. She placed the tray on the table just as Jackson appeared in the doorway. The whole room seemed to shift or maybe it was her heart finally settling into place.

"Morning again." He grinned and strolled over to where she stood. Holding her steady with a look he lowered his head and gently kissed her still swollen lips. "Hmm. Just like I remembered."

She giggled and playfully poked his arm. "It hasn't been *that* long." She hooked her fingers along the edge of the towel that was tucked around his waist.

"Long enough for me to recover." His large hands nearly encircled her waist and he realized how fragile her body was. He took her mouth with his own and savored again the sweetness of her tongue playing with his. He backed her up against the counter teasing the underside of her breasts with his thumbs. He nuzzled down her neck, pushing aside the folds of her robe. "Hmm. You make me crazy," he groaned before taking a dark nipple into his mouth.

Zoe's knees wobbled and she felt the inside of her thighs tremble. Jackson tugged on the belt that held her robe closed and practically tore it from her body. His hunger for her flashed so quickly and with such urgency that he was oblivious to where they were. All he knew was that he wanted her. *Now.*

He pushed his towel away, tossed it on the floor and lifted Zoe into his arms. She wrapped her legs above his hips and laced her fingers behind his head an instant before he rammed inside her with such force that starbursts flashed behind her eyes.

She buried her face in his neck to keep from screaming. The intensity of his thrusts drove her rapidly to the edge and there was nothing she could do to hold back the inevitable. She was coming hard and fast.

And so was he.

It was nearly noon by the time Zoe and Jackson got themselves together and settled on a truce to stay at least five feet away from each other until they got this crazy lust thing under control.

"How about we kiss to make it official," Jackson teased, finishing up his second shower of the morning. He shoved his arms into the sleeves of his shirt.

"Uh, no, I don't think so, buddy." Her cat was still purring and she didn't dare risk him coming anywhere near her anytime soon. She twisted her hair on top of her head and tied the string on her sweatpants into a knot, not that a simple knot would stop him if he really decided to get back inside her pants, so to speak.

To seal the deal they sat on opposite sides of Zoe's couch intermittently stealing glances at each other and laughing like fools as they finished up brunch and watched *Intimate Betrayal,* a made-for-television movie.

When the movie was over, Jackson helped clean up the kitchen and kept his promise to keep his hands and body to himself.

"So how long do you think your sister will be staying with you?" Zoe asked as she put one of the glasses into the overhead cabinet.

While they lay in bed earlier that morning, they'd found themselves whispering into the morning light about the importance of family—good or bad—and the impact they have on your life.

Zoe told him bits and pieces about growing up in a house full of women and that most of her life was spent under her grandmother's care because her mother wanted to pursue her singing career. She said she'd been an only child until she met Sharlene, who became like a sister to her. And Jackson found himself telling her about Michelle, how close they

An Important Message from the Publisher

Dear Reader,

Because you've chosen to read one of our fine novels, I'd like to say "thank you"! And, as a special way to say thank you, I'm offering to send you two more Kimani™ Romance novels and two surprise gifts—absolutely FREE! These books will keep it real with true-to-life African American characters that turn up the heat and sizzle with passion.

Please enjoy the free books and gifts with our compliments...

Glenda Howard

For Kimani Press™

Peel off Seal and

Place Inside...

We'd like to send you two free books to introduce you to Kimani™ Romance books. These novels feature strong, sexy women, and African-American heroes that are charming, loving and true. Our authors fill each page with exceptional dialogue, exciting plot twists, and enough sizzling romance to keep you riveted until the very end!

KIMANI ROMANCE...LOVE'S ULTIMATE DESTINATION

Your two books ha combined cover pr of $12.50 in the U.S $14.50 in Canada, b are yours **FREE!**

We'll even send you two wonderful surprise gifts. You can't lose!

THE EDITOR'S "THANK YOU" FREE GIFTS INCLUDE:

Two Kimani™ Romance Novels
Two exciting surprise gifts

YES! I have placed my Editor's "thank you" Free Gifts seal in the space provided at right. Please send me 2 FREE Books, and my 2 FREE Mystery Gifts. I understand that I am under no obligation to purchase anything further, as explained on the back of this card.

PLACE FREE GIFTS SEAL HERE

168/368 XDL FJKD

Please Print

FIRST NAME

LAST NAME

ADDRESS

APT.#   CITY

STATE/PROV.   ZIP/POSTAL CODE

Thank You!

The Reader Service - Here's How It Works:

Accepting your 2 free books and 2 free gifts (gifts valued at approximately $10.00) places you under no obligation to buy anything. You may keep the books and gifts and return the shipping statement marked "cancel." If you do not cancel, about a month later we'll send you 4 additional books and bill you just $4.94 each in the U.S. or $5.49 each in Canada. That is a savings of at least 21% off the cover price. Shipping and handling is just 50¢ per book in the U.S. and 75¢ per book in Canada.* You may cancel at any time, but if you choose to continue, every month we'll send you 4 more books, which you may either purchase at the discount price or return to us and cancel your subscription.
*Terms and prices subject to change without notice. Prices do not include applicable taxes. Sales tax applicable in N.Y. Canadian residents will be charged applicable taxes. Offer not valid in Quebec. All orders subject to credit approval. Credit or debit balances in a customer's account(s) may be offset by any other outstanding balance owed by or to the customer. Offer available while quantities last. Books received may not be as shown. Please allow 4 to 6 weeks for delivery.

If offer card is missing write to: The Reader Service, P.O. Box 1867, Buffalo, NY 14240-1867 or visit www.ReaderService.com

BUSINESS REPLY MAIL
FIRST-CLASS MAIL   PERMIT NO. 717   BUFFALO, NY

POSTAGE WILL BE PAID BY ADDRESSEE

THE READER SERVICE
PO BOX 1867
BUFFALO NY 14240-9952

NO POSTAGE
NECESSARY
IF MAILED
IN THE
UNITED STATES

had always been and how hurt and angry he was about what her husband Trevor had done.

"You were engaged?" Zoe asked, more curious than concerned.

"Yeah, for about a year."

"And your ex slept with your sister's husband."

He nodded, the anger beginning to brew again. He rinsed the last dish and placed it in the rack.

"She deserves jail time for that one," Zoe said and meant it. She couldn't imagine that kind of betrayal. "Right out of a *Jerry Springer* show."

Jackson couldn't help but laugh at that. "I know. Totally over the top." He shook his head slowly. "I always believed that Michelle and Travis would be forever. They were the couple to emulate. I introduced them." He blew out a breath. "And Carla, it never occurred to me that she was capable…"

Zoe touched his shoulder. "You can't blame yourself. It's messy, but they are all adults. You do what you need to for your sister, but don't take on that guilt. It won't help her or you."

His mouth formed a tight smile. "I could listen to your advice all day. How'd you get so wise?"

She grinned. "My Nana."

"You talk about her with such reverence. Every time you mention her name, your face lights up."

She dropped her gaze for a moment. "She means the world to me."

"I'd like to meet her one day."

Zoe's eyes traveled over his face, looking beyond

the surface, and saw the essence of the man and felt the goodness of his soul within her own. "I'd like that, too," she softly said.

Chapter 15

Zoe walked Jackson to the front door. She leaned against the doorframe and took in his image set against the backdrop of the setting sun. Since yesterday evening they hadn't been out of each other's sight or reach. Zoe felt as if something inside of her was separating, leaving a hollow emptiness.

Jackson brushed his thumb across her bottom lip. "I'll call you when I get in."

"Okay," she said, her voice sounding fragile as fine china.

"You okay?"

She pressed her lips together and wrapped her arms protectively around her waist. "Um, ummm."

"I'll just pick up a few things, check on Michelle

and Shay then head back. We can catch that film you wanted to see." His brow creased in concern. He gently clasped her upper arms. "Tell me what's wrong."

"I...I don't know. Just a feeling." Zoe looked into his eyes. "A feeling I've never had before," she said, her voice soft and dreamlike.

"Get your jacket and purse and whatever else you women take on the spur of the moment."

She laughed. "What?"

"You're coming with me. I think you'll like my sister. Besides I can rub your thigh on the drive over."

She swatted his arm and leaned up for a quick kiss. "Be right back."

"You sure your sister will be okay with me popping in, I mean with all that she has going on?"

Jackson glanced at her quickly as he maneuvered around a slow moving car. "Michelle is one of the friendliest people I know. And I'm not just saying that because she's my sister. Besides, she knows about you."

Zoe sat straight up in her seat. "Knows about me?" she cried. "What do you mean?"

He slowed to a red light. "This is going to sound crazy." He exhaled. "I'd been having dreams about a woman." He threw her a quick look. "They started getting stronger. And there was a growing sensation that I had to change my life, that there was something else out there waiting for me. I knew that I wasn't going to find it in New Orleans or with Carla."

The light turned green. He drove through the intersection and turned onto his street.

Zoe tried to make sense of what Jackson was saying. "A dream brought you here?" Her heart began to pound.

"I told you it sounds crazy. Forget it." He chuckled nervously.

"Did you see the woman's face?" she asked with trepidation, her thoughts running rampant.

"No. Not really. But I felt that I knew her."

The hair on her arms began to tingle. "How long ago did the dreams begin?"

"About a year ago, give or take a month."

Her stomach clenched. Her dreams had begun about that time as well.

He brought the car to a stop in front of a small town house. He turned halfway in his seat toward Zoe. "The only person I've told besides you is Michelle. I told her you were the woman in my dream. I knew it the instant I saw you that morning."

Zoe's breathing hitched. All of the foreshadowing, the legend was coming to pass. She couldn't ignore it or pretend it was just a bunch of stories handed down among heartbroken women to explain away their unhappiness. But if that was true—then so was the rest.

"See, I've freaked you out."

Zoe blinked back to the here and now and looked into Jackson's eyes. She smiled softly. "Once you meet my family, you'll realize that you'll have to do better than that to freak me out."

Jackson blew out a sigh of relief then leaned across the car to share a quick kiss. "Ready?"

"Yep."

"I'm so glad to finally meet you," Michelle said as she shook Zoe's hand then pulled her into a quick hug. "Jackson has been telling me all about you— well, not *all* about you," she said over her laughter. "Oh, and I can't thank you enough for looking after Shay the other night."

Zoe liked Michelle immediately. For a woman who was dealing with her own drama, she was warm and bubbly and genuinely sincere. And she could tell from the looks that she flashed in Jackson's direction that she adored her brother.

Michelle was also tall and slender and had the same deep dark eyes and strong features as her brother. There was no mistaking that they were siblings.

"He's told me about you as well."

"Mommy, that's the lady who found me."

Michelle picked Shay up and propped her on her hip. "Yep, and she came to say hello."

"Hi."

"Hello, Shay. You haven't been doing any wandering around, have you?"

"No," she said, shaking her head vigorously back and forth.

Zoe winked. "Good girl."

"Can I get you anything?" Michelle asked.

"No, I'm good."

"I was just starting dinner. You are staying for dinner, right?" Her tapered brows rose.

Zoe turned to look at Jackson, who nonchalantly shrugged.

"Sure. Can I help?"

"I never turn down help. Hope you like baked salmon."

"Love it," she said following Michelle and Shay into the kitchen.

While the ladies were busy in the kitchen, Jackson went up to his bedroom to change clothes, but he had a feeling that they wouldn't be going anywhere. Once Michelle got to talking there was no stopping her. He smiled and opened his closet door. Zoe might just be the medicine that Michelle needed. She could use a friend, especially now.

"So how long have you lived in Atlanta?"

"Just about five years. I came here from New Orleans."

"You're kidding!" She spun toward her, holding a piece of salmon in her hand. "We grew up in New Orleans."

"I know," Zoe said over her laughter. "It's crazy that we never met."

"Where did you go to school?"

"Montclair High School and then the University of New Orleans. I came to New York for grad school then moved back home, then here."

"I've never lived anywhere other than New Orleans. Everything I know is there," Michelle said, her voice losing its vitality. She turned back toward the sink.

"Atlanta is a wonderful city. Full of history, nightlife, places to eat, great schools, good people."

Michelle was quiet then talked with her back still turned. "Did Jackson tell you why I'm here?"

Zoe wasn't sure how much she should admit to. Was Jackson breaking a confidence by telling her? "Um…not a lot." She sliced and diced tomatoes and added them to the spinach in a large glass bowl.

"It's okay if he did. I trust my brother's judgment." She paused and sprinkled some black pepper on the salmon and then squeezed lemon juice over them. "I'm kind of at a loss right now. I feel like I'm in some kind of limbo." Her voice began to wobble.

Zoe felt her pain right in the center of her chest. She couldn't imagine that kind of betrayal, from not one but two people who you trusted. She got up from her seat at the table and came to stand alongside Michelle at the sink.

"Limbo is probably where you need to be right now. Just for a little while," she added, when Michelle turned a stunned look on her. She gently touched her arm. "Give yourself some time. Time to be angry, sad, confused, hurt, whatever it takes and then you put one foot in front of the other and move forward."

Michelle's eyes were watery as her tears cascaded over her lashes. She sniffed and wiped her eyes with the back of her hand. "I just…" Her slender shoulders heaved and she broke down and sobbed.

Zoe gathered her in her arms and held her close, whispering soothing words, telling her that it would be all right. Jackson appeared in the doorway and stopped short. Zoe looked at him over Michelle's shoulder and mouthed that it was all right. He quietly turned and left.

"I feel so silly crying all over you and we just met." She sniffed and sputtered a nervous laugh.

"As long as you don't get all those salty tears all over that salmon," Zoe teased.

Michelle giggled self-consciously and wiped her eyes. She blinked back the rest of her tears and focused on Zoe. "Thank you."

"I didn't do anything."

"I see why Jackson is with you. You're a very special woman."

"Mommy! I'm hungry," Shay said, bursting into the kitchen.

The two women turned to Shay then looked at each other and knew that they'd found a new friend.

* * *

"Dinner was delicious," Jackson said, wiping his mouth with a paper napkin. "I could get used this."

"Don't," Michelle said, beginning to pick up empty plates from the table.

"I told Michelle that as long as she was going to be here for a little while, if she wanted to stay busy we have a part-time opening for a docent at the museum."

Jackson's brow rose. He looked from one face to the other. "Really?"

"I haven't decided yet, but I'm thinking about it. I mean there are things that I need to take care of first, back home."

"Whatever you decide to do, sis, you know I'm behind you one hundred percent."

"Whenever you're ready," Zoe added.

Jackson checked his watch. "If you still want to catch that movie, we need to leave to make the last show."

Zoe stretched and covered a yawn with her hand. "Hmm, maybe I should take a raincheck on that. I have to be in the office early tomorrow."

"I'll drive you home."

Zoe put the last of the dishes in the dishwasher. "Great dinner, Michelle." She lightly kissed her cheek. "Next time dinner is on me."

"I'll be there. And thank you," she added for only Zoe to hear.

"Don't even think about it. And call me. We can

have lunch. I'd love for you to meet my friend Sharlene."

"I will. Night."

Zoe followed Jackson out of the kitchen, said good-night to Shay who was drifting off to sleep on the couch and walked out into the balmy spring night.

"You and Michelle really seemed to hit it off. I kinda knew you would." He opened the passenger door to the Explorer.

"Did you?" She grinned and hopped in.

Jackson came around and got in. "She could use a friend. And that was really nice of you to offer her a job."

"Our tour guides are mostly students, so they come and go. It's easy work. Great hours and it will take her mind off of her own problems for a while." She fastened her seat belt. "Has she said what she plans to do about her husband?"

He turned the key in the ignition. His jaw clenched. "No, not really. I think she's still in shock. I know I am. I want her to relax for a while before she even thinks about dealing with Travis." His head snapped toward her. "You know the bastard didn't even call." He slammed his palm against the steering wheel.

Zoe reached out and covered his clenched fist with her hand. "She's going to come through this."

He lifted his gaze. "Yeah. But she shouldn't have

to go through it at all." He put the truck in gear and pulled off.

Shortly after, Jackson and Zoe pulled up in front of her house. He cut off the engine.

"This has been an amazing two days. I feel as if I've known you so much longer."

"I know. I feel the same way." He reached across and rested his hand against the back of neck.

She sighed softly. "Don't go home," she said, capturing his hand. "Stay with me tonight."

"Do you promise to keep your hands and body to yourself and let me sleep undisturbed?"

She grinned. "No."

"Now that's what I wanted to hear." He kissed her softly and they went inside.

Chapter 16

"Where have you been? I've been calling you for two days! I started to come over there, but then I figured I might interrupt something," Sharlene said. "I should be pissed that you didn't call your best friend in the whole world and tell her every intimate detail."

Zoe bit back her grin. "If you give me half a minute I'll tell you."

"Did you actually turn off your phone?"

"Yes."

"Damn. It was like that?"

"All that and more," Zoe said dreamily. "I don't know where to begin."

"At the beginning!"

Zoe laughed. "Over lunch."

Sharlene huffed. "Fine. I'll see if I can squeeze you in."

"You betta. Two o'clock. I'll meet you at your office. Gotta run."

"See you later."

Zoe hung up the phone and it rang again. "Zoe Beaumont," she said without checking the caller ID.

"Baby."

"Mom?" She sat up. "What's wrong? Is it Nana?"

"Nothing's wrong. She wants to talk to you and she insisted that I call your job. Hang on."

Zoe briefly closed her eyes in relief and her racing heart slowed.

"Zoe."

"Nana. Hi. How are you?"

"I'm fine, better now that I hear your voice."

Zoe relaxed against the chair. "This is a treat. You never call me at work."

"He's in your life now, sweetheart."

Her pulse kicked up again. "How do you know that?"

Nana chuckled. "The same way I know everything. I got the gift, just like you. When you gonna bring the boy to see me?"

Zoe's eyes widened. "Nana, I just met him. Can I get used to him first before I spring the family on him?"

"Don't wait too long. There's not a lot of time. Your birthday is coming."

"I know. And I'll turn thirty just like anyone else."

Nana chuckled. "Here's your mama."

Zoe listened to the shuffling, clicking and background noises as the phone was passed to her mother.

"Hey, sweetie, listen I wanted to do something really special for your birthday."

"Ma, really you don't have to. I—"

"No, I do and I want to." She paused for a beat. "There's so much that I've missed in your life, Zoe. So many birthdays and school trips and first dates. It would mean so much to me if you would let me do this one thing for you."

It was true. Everything that her mother said was true. For years their relationship had been less than ideal and for most of her growing up years her mother played no real part in her life. They'd made amends to a degree. She loved her mother but there was a part of her that still resented that her mother thought of her second instead of first. It made it even more difficult for her to feel secure in any relationship.

"Please, Zoe. It will be fun and tasteful."

"Nothing too extravagant," she said finally conceding.

"Of course not."

Zoe shut her eyes and laughed lightly. She knew what that meant—horse-drawn carriages, fire-eating entertainers, magicians and acrobats. "Don't embarrass me," she playfully warned.

"I wouldn't dare. And you are going to bring him with you." It was more statement than question.

"Him?"

"We all talked about it."

"We? Who is we?"

"Your grandmother, your aunts and me."

"What did you talk about?" she hesitantly asked.

"That it had taken all these years and four generations, but this time, this time the legacy will be fulfilled—by you."

"Ma," she breathed. "I don't want to be the one responsible for everyone else's happiness. I can barely manage my own. And I don't want you and Nana and Aunt Fern and Aunt Flo to depend on that and then be disappointed."

"We won't be," she said, confident in her pronouncement. "Well, you get back to work. And I'm going to start preparing for a party! Goodbye, sweetheart." She disconnected the call.

Zoe flopped back in her chair. "A party." A slow smile tugged the corners of her mouth.

"What happened to you Friday night?" Jackson asked, striding alongside Levi as they headed down the corridor toward their respective classes.

"Man, I had every intention of coming. I went home, sat on the couch and that was the last thing I remember. Out like a light." He chuckled.

"Not as young as you used to be, man. You can't be burning it on both ends."

"I know. As soon as this dissertation is presented on Wednesday I can take a breather and the semester will be over. Think I'll take a trip somewhere and just chill."

"You're gonna need it." As much as Levi pretended to be a hound with a laundry list of women, he was really a hardworking, driven man who was actually pretty old-fashioned when it came to relationships.

"So how was it?"

"Crowded. I think the class enjoyed it, though. I'll find out in a few."

"You look like you have an extra pep in your step this morning. What's up?" he asked conspiratorially. He lightly nudged him with his elbow.

"It's all good," he said evading the real question that he wasn't quite ready to discuss.

Levi shrugged. "Cool."

They reached the fork in the corridor.

"Catch up with you later, man," Levi said.

"Yeah, have a good one. Listen, Lee, I was thinking about throwing some steaks on the grill this Saturday. Why don't you swing by?"

He grinned. "Free food. I'm there."

"We can celebrate your new PhD. Dr. Dr."

"Thanks, man." He adjusted his designer glasses. "Let me know what I need to bring."

"Just bring yourself. The night's on me."

"Cool. We'll talk."

They gave each other some dap and turned off in opposite directions.

It had been a while since he'd had real guests at his place or thrown a party. He would definitely have to get Michelle involved. Dinner parties were right up her alley and it would give her something to do and keep her mind off of Travis.

At some point, he was going to have to go down there and deal with Travis and so was Michelle. He cringed every time he thought about the whole sordid mess. And to think that at one time he actually thought he was going to marry Carla and make a life with her. He didn't even know her.

Jackson approached his classroom and was surprised to see Victoria standing in the hallway. She was busy talking on her cell phone and he didn't think she noticed him. So much had happened over the weekend that he hadn't had a chance to process what she'd told him. He started to approach her but she started off down the hall and was quickly swept up in the rush of students heading to classes. Meanwhile he didn't know who she was talking about and he still needed an assistant. He opened the door to the lecture hall and took his place at the head of the class.

Victoria pushed through the exit doors and stepped outside, heading for the parking lot.

"I said I'm done. It's not right. I should have never agreed in the first place. You need to move on." She used the remote and unlocked the car door and got in. Victoria took one look back at the campus, stuck the key in the ignition and drove off.

"Hey, Mike!"

Mike stopped halfway up the staircase then came back down. He crossed the main floor to where Zoe was walking toward him.

"Hey. I hope we are proud of ourselves," he said with a grin.

"*We* certainly are. I wanted to thank you for all of your help. The opening was spectacular."

"Just following directions, boss. I gotta check on a delivery. Need anything?"

"No. Back to writing some grants. So I'll be in my office most of the day."

He nodded and started to walk off.

"So how is everything with, uh, you and Linda? Things working out with the scheduling and all?" She held her leather portfolio up against her chest.

He eyed her for a moment. "Yeah, everything's good. Why? Did she say something?"

"No," she squeaked in a voice she didn't quite recognize. "I was only wondering."

"Oh."

"Anyway, let me get busy. See you later," she said a bit too quickly and walked off. *That went over well. I should have simply confessed what I knew for all the subtlety that moment lacked.*

Her cell phone chirped. She took it from the tiny

pouch on her waist and checked the lighted face. Her heart leaped. "Hey, Jack," she said, her voice taking on a husky tone.

"Just finished up with my class and I wanted to hear your voice. How's your day going so far?"

"I'm glad you called." She opened her office door and closed it behind her.

"How glad?"

She giggled. "Hmm, maybe I can count the ways later this evening."

"Those are the kind of numbers I like to hear. I'll go home, grab some things and come by around seven?"

"Perfect. I'll see you then."

"Enjoy your day."

"I already am," she said softly. "See you at seven."

Zoe floated through her morning with a smile on her face, breezing through the painstaking details needed for the grant that she was working on. By the time she looked up she realized she had about five minutes to meet Sharlene. She saved the data on the computer and shut it down, grabbed her purse and just as she was on her way out her office phone rang. She started to let it go to voice mail, but at the last second she picked it up.

"Zoe Beaumont."

"Good afternoon, Ms. Beaumont. This is Eric Lang."

"Oh, Mr. Lang." She came back around her desk and sat. "What can I do for you?" she asked, hoping that it was anything other than what he'd asked about the other night.

"I was hoping you could make some time in your schedule to meet with several members from the Guggenheim. They want to talk to you about the exhibit and what your responsibilities will be."

"*Will* be? I haven't agreed that I would go to New York," she said with caution. "I thought I was going to have time to think about it and make a decision."

"The Guggenheim members are very anxious to meet with you. They'll only be here until tomorrow afternoon. I told them that tomorrow morning at ten would be fine. We can use the conference room."

"Mr. Lang, this isn't what we discussed."

"There is a lot on the line here, Ms. Beaumont. I'm sure your job and the work you do is just as important to you as it is to the High."

She flinched. What was going on?

"Looking forward to our meeting tomorrow." He disconnected the call.

Dazed, Zoe returned the receiver to the base. Was Lang trying to tell her that she had no choice in the matter? What if she decided that she wasn't going? Would she lose her job?

Her cell phone chirped.

"You still coming?" Sharlene's voice and the background noise of the street came through the phone.

"Sorry. Something came up. I'm walking out of the door now."

"Hey, what's wrong?"

"I'll tell you about when I get there."

"Move to New York? Why you?"

"I have no idea. But he made it sound like I didn't have a choice."

Sharlene set her purse down beside her on the bench. "Doesn't make sense. You're doing a great job. Aren't you?"

Zoe threw her a look.

"Sorry," she droned. "I'm just saying…if you're doing a good job, why hand you off to another museum?"

Zoe dipped her spoon into her yogurt and took a thoughtful mouthful. "That's the million dollar question." She sighed. "Not much I can do about it until I hear what they have to say tomorrow."

They were quiet for a moment.

"Guess your mind isn't on telling me about your weekend," Sharlene hedged.

Zoe grinned. "Well, since you twisted my arm…"

She left out some of the intimate, intimate details, figuring she'd leave those up to Sharlene's very vivid imagination. But she did share the mind-blowing experience of feeling transported back in time.

Sharlene stared in stunned amazement. "Wow."

"Yeah, wow. I don't know what to make of it." She took another spoonful of yogurt.

"You talk to Nana about it?"

"Sharl! Do you really think I'm going to tell my ninety-something-year-old grandmother about my sexcapade with a man I just met?"

"I'm just saying."

Zoe slowly shook her head. "My mother wants to throw me a birthday party," she said switching gears.

"Wait, *your* mother, Miraya Beaumont?"

"Can you believe it?"

"Maybe she's trying to make up for all the ones she missed. This *is* supposed to be the big one for you."

"Maybe."

"Gosh, it's hot out here today. Imagine what the summer is going to be like. We'll have to be in bathing suits at your birthday party."

Zoe laughed. "Weather is crazy all over. I wish my mother would convince Nana and my aunts to move farther inland. They were lucky these past few times with the hurricanes and the flooding, but some of their neighbors weren't."

"You know good and well that Nana is not giving up that house. And neither will your aunts. Besides, that house has too much family history, Zee."

"I know. But I just worry about them." She checked her watch and jumped up. "I gotta get back."

Sharlene touched Zoe's hand. "Everything is going to work out. See what they have to say tomorrow and take it from there."

"Yeah," she conceded. She leaned over and kissed Sharlene's cheek. "I'll call you."

"When am I going to meet Mr. Wonderful?"

"Soon." She winked and hurried off.

Chapter 17

Zoe had just gotten out of the shower and into some comfy gray sweatpants and a white T-shirt when the front doorbell rang. Jackson was just the remedy she needed after that unsettling phone call from Lang, she thought. She stuck her feet in a pair of flip-flops and went to the door. She peeked through the curtains covering the side window. Her insides smiled when she saw Jackson standing on the porch with a huge bouquet of flowers. Quickly she opened the door and immediately found herself wrapped in his arms and her mouth covered with his.

She moaned against his lips, oblivious to the fact that they were standing in her doorway, making out like two teenagers.

"Hmm, just as sweet as I remember," he said against her lips.

"Are those for me?" she asked, taking his free hand and leading him inside.

"Absolutely. Where should I put them?"

"I'll get a vase." She took the flowers, gave him a quick kiss and went into the kitchen for a vase.

"Something smells good," he said, following her into the kitchen.

"Roast chicken."

"Can I help with anything?"

She reached up and took a vase down from the top shelf of one of the cabinets. "Hmm, don't think so. Everything is almost finished. Want something to drink?"

"What do you have?"

"Hard or soft?"

He gave a half grin. "That's a loaded question that I could answer one of two ways."

Zoe put her hand on her hip and her right brow arched. "Okay, let me rephrase. Are you thirsty?"

He walked slowly over to her, dipped his head and brushed his lips across her neck.

She shivered, delighting in the heat he stirred. "You're making this very difficult," she said, her words catching in her throat when his tongue flicked along the soft skin of her neck. "We'll never have dinner if you keep that up."

He gave her one last kiss. "I would hate for you

to have gone to all this trouble for no reason," he said, backing off with a wicked smile on his face.

Zoe laughed. "I have some of that raspberry rum. Can I fix you a glass?"

"Show me where you hide your stash and I'll fix one for both of us."

"Living room, in the cabinet, under the television."

"Be right back."

Jackson sauntered out and Zoe added a capful of olive oil to a pot of boiling water. She added fresh string beans and diced red pepper to the pot, lowered the flame and covered it. The seasoned yellow rice was simmering and the chicken was almost done. She listened to Jackson humming in the living room. It would be so easy to totally give in and let go—just feel. According to Nana, everything in her life had been leading to this time. But logic resisted and her heart remained wary.

"What do you want to mix with this?" Jackson asked, holding up the bottle.

Zoe turned from the stove, storing her thoughts away as she wiped her hands on a black and white striped kitchen towel. She put it down on the granite counter. "Hmm, iced tea works for me. You know where the glasses are." She turned off the flame under the rice.

"Do you always cook like this in the middle of the week?"

"Actually, no. I'm trying to impress you."

"Is that right?" He put some crushed ice from the dispenser on the fridge in the glasses, splashed the rum over the ice then added the iced tea. He handed her a glass. "I was impressed a long time ago." He tapped his glass against hers.

She took a sip and then looked at him above the rim of her glass. "If I would have known that, I would have ordered Domino's instead."

Jackson sputtered. "No more compliments for you."

Zoe laughed. "Dinner is almost done. Do you want to eat inside or outside?"

"I vote for out back."

"Okay. Can you get the plates? I'll clean off the table."

They worked in tandem, adding and subtracting what they needed for their dinner under the stars. Shortly they settled down and dug in. Music from the stereo filtered out onto the deck and votive scented candles on the railing gave the whole area a soothing setting.

"Humph, delicious," Jackson said, finishing off his last forkful of seasoned rice.

"Old family recipe. Had enough?"

"I'm stuffed."

Zoe started to get up and clear the table. Jackson covered her hand to stop her. She gave him a questioning look.

"Sit, relax for a minute. We can do that later. How was your day?"

She laughed at the clichéd line.

"What? Did I say something funny?"

"It just struck me as funny. Sounds like a conversation couples have after they've known each other for ages."

"Don't you feel like that sometimes?" He stared at her until she looked away.

"Sometimes," she finally admitted. "We really should get this stuff cleaned up, it's getting late." She jumped up from her seat before Jackson could stop her this time.

Jackson watched her walk away and instinctively knew that something was wrong. Maybe he needed to give her some space. Things were happening quickly between them, maybe too quickly for Zoe. He believed deep down in his gut that she was what he'd been waiting for, looking for and now that he'd found her he didn't want to waste a minute. Zoe didn't seem to feel the same way and being the very determined woman that she was, he knew pushing her when she wasn't ready wouldn't work. Even though they'd shared their bodies in the most intimate ways and experienced something that had never happened to either of them, he knew that Zoe had not shared her heart. He brought the last of the dishes into the kitchen.

Zoe was loading the dishwasher and putting leftovers into plastic containers. She gave him a short glance.

"Did I tell you that I lost my teaching assistant?"

She snapped a blue plastic lid onto a container. "No, what happened?"

"That's the crazy part, I'm not sure."

She put the containers in the fridge. Jackson turned on the dishwasher.

"I don't understand."

He leaned against the stove and crossed his arms. Zoe lowered herself into a chair and crossed her legs at the knee.

"Before the semester began, I'd put in for a teaching assistant to help with the research that I'm working on and to cover some of my classes if necessary. Fast forward, I got Victoria. I had my issues with her in the beginning, but she actually seemed to work out—as far as her work was concerned. So I tried to put aside the fact that she was a little *too* eager."

"Too eager. What do you mean?"

He told her about her enthusiasm to go above and beyond what was required for her position.

"Like what?"

"It's hard to explain. On the surface it doesn't seem like anything, the extra hours, always prompt always *there*." He looked at Zoe hoping that she understood what he was making a mess of explaining. "It started making me uncomfortable."

It took Zoe a minute and then her brows rose in understanding. "Ohhh."

"The thing is I was completely wrong." He went on to tell her about Victoria coming to him and telling him that she was leaving and then showing up at his door.

"Someone at the college is trying to screw up your chances at getting the department chair? But why? And who?"

He slowly shook his head. "I have no idea."

Zoe got up and came to stand in front of him. "Maybe it's all just some crazy drama she cooked up. Maybe she really did, or rather does have feelings for you and this was her way out." Her gaze glided over his constricted expression. She stroked his cheek. "You have no reason to believe that there is some ulterior motive on the part of one of your colleagues—just the word of a teaching assistant who didn't give you any proof whatsoever."

He took her hand and kissed the inside of her palm. "You're probably right."

"I had a pretty strange day today."

"What happened?"

"I got a call from my mother."

He laughed. "Is that strange?"

"Humph, you don't know my mother," she said.

"Okay, you got me on that one. So what happened?"

They walked together into the living room and sat down on the couch. Zoe tucked her feet under her and rested her arm on the couch back.

"She wants to give me a birthday party."

Jackson frowned in confusion. "Hmm, and that's a bad thing?"

"Not a bad thing, just a weird thing." She sighed trying to get her thoughts in order so that she didn't come off as some ungrateful daughter. "My mother and I haven't always had the best relationship. To be honest, we didn't have one at all until a few years ago." She rested her head in her palm. "My grandmother raised me while my mother 'toured' the country singing." She shrugged slightly. "I didn't know her. She was just this woman who showed up every few months in fancy clothes, brought gifts and then went off again. She was never there. She wasn't there for school trips or when I acted in my first play. She didn't sign report cards or tell me about boys. She missed my senior prom, birthdays, holidays. Oh, she'd send a card or a present from wherever she was at the time, but…"

"You wanted *her,*" he said softly. He stroked her hair.

She felt her throat tightening and her eyes begin to burn, which surprised her. She thought she'd long ago put all those feelings to rest.

"When she came back for the last time, we were practically strangers. She had no idea what I liked or disliked or even what I did for a living." She glanced away. "My grandmother told me that I had to be the bigger person and to give her a chance. We all deserve a second chance, she said. So, I tried. And over the years we've moved from strangers to acquaintances. There's no way she can catch up on all the years that she missed."

Jackson took it all in, heard the hurt in her voice that she tried to hide. But she couldn't. It was in the words that she *didn't* say. It was in her eyes. She wanted her mother's love, as any child does no matter how old they are. And at the same time she was rejecting that love because it had done nothing but hurt and disappoint her all of her life.

"Are you afraid to care because you think she might leave again or not live up to your expectations?" he asked gently.

She looked into his eyes, seeing the compassion there. She bit down on her lip to keep from crying. How could he know what was in her heart? But of course he would.

"It's made you cautious. It's made you hesitate to open your heart completely. Everyone is not like your mother, Zoe. Your grandmother proved that."

"But if you love someone, how can you just leave them?"

He gently toyed with a few strands of her hair. "I wish I knew. People are complicated."

"You got that right," she said drolly.

"And some things you can never explain. They just are."

"You're sounding very philosophical."

His eyes crinkled at the corners. "It was my second major."

Zoe's mouth dropped open in surprise. "You're kidding?"

"Nope. Double major, Art History and Philosophy."

She bobbed her head in admiration. "Great combination! I'm sure understanding the thinking during a certain period in time and among groups of people helps immensely in relating to the art."

"Absolutely. And in life. It's all relevant. But back to this party... I'm always looking for a reason." He moved a little closer. "What do you want for your birthday?"

Zoe glanced up slightly, catching the supportive look in his eyes. All she wanted was to stop being afraid to believe. "Nothing special. I'm easy."

They spent the rest of the evening talking, laughing, listening to music and sharing stories about their childhood growing up in New Orleans, still amazed that they'd lived so close to each other and had never met.

"We went to the same school in N.O. I was just ahead of you by a few years," Jackson said.

"Exactly, by the time I got to Montclair you were out. Besides, even if we were in school at the same time, you wouldn't have paid me any attention."

"And why not?"

"Trust me, I was long and lanky, no meat on my bones. My knees used to knock when I walked. My grandmother use to braid my hair in a million braids, and I had braces until I was sixteen." She chuckled at the memories. "I was a hot mess."

She popped up from the couch and went to the end table. Underneath was an album. She pulled it off the shelf and came back to sit beside Jackson. She flipped the book open until she found the picture she was looking for.

"That's me in the middle."

She pointed to a reed-thin girl in hot-pink shorts with the knobbiest knees he'd ever seen, a head full of thick black hair and braces that were obvious when she smiled into the camera. The black-rimmed glasses were the icing on the cake. She was standing between two elegant older women, the color of honey, dolled up in wide-brimmed Sunday-go-to-meeting hats and pastel dresses.

It took all of his good home-training not to crack up laughing. "This is you?" he asked, in equal parts question and accusation.

"Yep." Zoe pinched her lips together to keep from snickering.

"Wow," he managed. "You were a cute kid."

She slugged him in the arm. "Stop lying."

He howled with laughter. "Let's see some more."

She slowly turned the pages, pointing herself out at her different stages of awkward development. "This is Aunt Flo, she's the oldest. And that's Aunt Fern."

There were dozens of photos of her and Sharlene from serious to comical during various stages of their growing up and friendship.

"Where's Nana?"

Zoe turned toward the back of the album that she had reserved for her grandmother.

Zora Beaumont was a stunning woman, regal-looking, Jackson observed. It was clear in her strong African features, the smooth dark skin taut over prominent cheekbones and full lips, and her bold but sharp nose. Her daughters resembled her in degrees, each one possessing one or more of her features. But it was Zoe who was her incarnation—a young version of Zora.

"Beautiful woman," he said almost reverently as Zoe tenderly passed her hand across one of the photographs of her grandmother.

"Yes, inside and out."

"I'm looking forward to meeting her."

"She wants to meet you, too."

"You told her about us?" That surprised him.

"It was more like, *she* told me about *you*."

"Huh?"

"It's a long story, best told when you've had a few drinks," she said, wanting to dismiss the direction of the conversation. She wasn't ready to tell him about all the myths and legends and particularly what his role was supposed to be in it all. It's one thing to grow up with all that stuff. It was quite another to hear it from someone who'd just entered your life.

Jackson wanted her to tell him the long story. The one that he believed would explain so much of what had been happening to him and what had happened between him and Zoe.

He draped his arm around her shoulder and kissed the top of her head. "Well, if it helps any, you clean up real good. You've come a long way baby."

"Oh, very funny."

"I'm serious." He chuckled then he lifted her chin with the tip of his finger and looked into her eyes. "I'm serious," he said again, his voice lower this time touching her right in the center of her being.

Her face warmed by degrees.

Jackson brushed his lips against hers then teased their plumpness with the very tip of his tongue. He felt the slightest tremor run through her as he stroked her bare arm and urged her closer.

The instant her unbound breasts pressed up against the firmness of Jackson's chest, Zoe's insides ignited. Her nipples hardened and poked at the soft fabric of her T-shirt. They longed to be touched, the ache soothed.

She took Jackson's hand and covered her breast with it. He squeezed ever so gently and when she moaned in response he leaned her back against the couch so that she was partly beneath him. He pushed her T-shirt up exposing her breasts. Deep in his throat he made an unintelligible sound before laving the tempting sweet skin with his tongue.

Zoe's body arched while he suckled and tremors of need ran along the course of her limbs. She squeezed her hands between their bodies and pulled the strings of her sweatpants loose.

Jackson didn't need any more hints. He helped her out of her pants and almost came when he realized that all the time they'd been together for the evening she hadn't been wearing any panties. Overcome with wanting her, he grabbed her thighs and pulled her farther down on the couch before draping her legs over his shoulders so that he could taste her again.

His tongue was hot and wet and expert and Zoe's clit sang with joy and her insides shed warm tears that Jackson let slide over his lips. He parted her opening and then gently slid one finger inside of her. Her hips bucked. Two. She moaned. Three. Her body tensed. She gripped his shoulders. His tongue played hide and seek while his fingers moved in and out in a maddeningly slow rhythm.

Zoe's thighs widened. She tossed one leg across the back of the couch. Without losing a beat, Jackson undid his pants and got them down below his knees.

"Look at me," he demanded, his voice thick and raw.

Zoe's eyes fluttered open. Her breath rose and fell in short bursts.

"I want you. I want all of you. I don't want to fuck you. I want to make love to you. That's what I'm going to do," he whispered, positioning himself between her waiting thighs. "Is that all right with you?" He held his thick, long penis in his hand—waiting for her response.

"Yes," she gushed on a hot breath.

He pushed the head in.

Her head jerked to the side.

"Are you sure?"

She pushed her hips against him. He pulled back.

"Are you sure?"

"Yes!" She dug her fingers into his butt.

He thrust deeper.

"Ohhhh, God…"

"Sure…?"

"Yes, yes…" she cried as his thrusts went deeper, stayed longer, in and out, faster, slower, faster.

Jackson kissed and caressed her, ran his hands along her body, explored it, made it his.

Zoe wound her arms and her legs around him needing him beneath her skin, whimpering in ecstasy as he stroked her and stroked her, so deep, so deep.

Their hearts pounded in time with the sound of distant drums. Birds called into the night, rustling the trees against the blue-black sky. The ground shook. The flames in the fire pit rose, and it was done.

Zoe's heart thumped in her chest, refusing to slow down. It happened again—that out-of-body experience. It was like making love on some mind-altering drug. It was totally beyond her comprehension.

She didn't want to feel so vulnerable, so open and out of control. When she was with Jackson she didn't think clearly. She let her guard down, saying things and feeling things that she would rather not.

The flashbacks when they made love went against everything that she professed to believe in: going slow, no commitment and not allowing her emotions to rule her head.

Jackson draped his leg across her thigh. "You okay?"

"Hmm, umm."

He kissed the back of her neck, closed his eyes and inhaled her soft scent. He felt like he was on a roller coaster that was hurtling into the unknown. This inexplicable connection that he felt with Zoe he'd never experienced before. It was new and exciting and a little scary in its intensity. But somehow he knew it was right. He wouldn't rush her. He wouldn't pressure her. For now, he was going to go with the flow and let Zoe take the lead.

"I was planning a little get together at my place this weekend. I thought it would cheer up Michelle."

"Is that an invitation?" She turned over on her side to face him.

He trailed his finger down the bridge of her nose. "Yeah, it is."

"Is it okay if I bring a guest?"

"Sure. The more the merrier."

"Great. Then you'll get to meet Sharlene. You'll really like her."

"I'm sure I will." He pulled her closer and felt himself becoming aroused yet again.

"Is that for me?" she asked in a husky voice, her eyes darkening as they rolled over his face. She reached down to stroke him.

His jaw clenched. "For as long as you want it."

Chapter 18

"You've been quiet since we got up," Jackson said, pulling on his shirt.

Zoe sat on the edge of the bed and slipped her feet into her shoes. "Lots on my mind," she said in a monotone.

Jackson buttoned his shirt, all the while watching Zoe who'd been distant and distracted. He couldn't figure out why.

"I'm probably going to drive down to New Orleans next weekend to pick up some of Michelle's and Shay's things."

Her gaze jumped to him. "Really? Going to see Carla while you're there?" She stood and tugged on the hem of her navy blue suit jacket.

Jackson flinched at the accusatory tone. "I'm not going to see Carla." He crossed the bedroom to where she stood. "What's wrong?"

She turned her head away. "Nothing." Gently she pressed her hands against his chest. "I'm going to be late." She breezed by him, took her purse from the side chair and walked out of the bedroom.

"I'll call you later," Jackson said. He opened her car door for her.

"I'm going to be really busy today. If I get a break I'll give you a call. Okay?" She got in behind the wheel.

"Sure. Whenever you're ready." He shut the door and stepped away as she backed up and pulled out of the driveway without looking back.

Jackson stood in that spot for several moments until he lost sight of Zoe's car. Finally he got into his Explorer and pulled off.

Zoe pushed through the door of the museum and barely looked left or right as she crossed the marble floors. Frank, the security guard, called out, "Good morning." She didn't hear him.

There was no reason to act like such a witch to Jackson, she thought, unlocking her office door. He had no idea what was going on. And she didn't quite understand why she acted the way that she did, as if it was all his fault.

She took off her jacket and hung it on the coat rack. In a way it was his fault. If he wasn't in her life, if he hadn't stirred up feelings, awakened her lust for his touch, made her start thinking about the future that involved someone other than herself then she wouldn't give a second thought about going to New York. But that wasn't the case.

Swiveling her chair toward her computer she booted it up and waited for the High Museum of Art logo to fill the screen. She leaned her elbows on the desk and pressed her fist to her chin. Everything was happening too fast. She felt like she was being squeezed into a box not of her own making.

The dream last night was so intense that it woke her up several times. All night she was running from a storm. Everywhere she looked the sky was dark and ominous. Rain slashed so hard that she couldn't see in front of her. She sensed more than knew that she had to be somewhere. She had to get to *some*place. But every time she tried, the car stalled or she got lost, or was blinded by the rain. Her feet felt like they were being pulled down into quicksand. She heard herself yell for help, but nothing came out of her mouth. No one could hear her. It was a dream that she'd been having off and on for the past year. There were different versions of it with varying degrees of intensity. But always she was heading to some unknown destination.

She woke up exhausted and tense and her restless night was met with this meeting in less than a half hour. She couldn't even think straight. Resting her head in her palm she briefly shut her eyes. What was happening to her?

Zoe jumped with a start at the sound of her phone ringing. She shook her head in confusion. She grabbed the receiver, blinking rapidly to clear her vision.

"Yes. Zoe Beaumont."

"Ms. Beaumont, the chairman is waiting for you in the conference room."

She squinted at her watch. Ten twenty-five!

"I'll be right there. Thank you."

She stood. Had she actually fallen asleep at her desk? That had never happened before. She hurried across the room and snatched her jacket from the hook then darted back to her desk and took her compact out from her purse. She checked her reflection then freshened up her lipstick. She actually felt woozy.

Drawing in a long calming breath, she put on her jacket and walked out.

When Zoe reached the conference room, the visitors from the Guggenheim along with Chairman Lang and several of the board members of the High Museum were already in place, some drinking coffee.

"Well, good morning, Ms. Beaumont," Eric Lang said. "Please come in and join us. We were waiting for you."

She looked around the room, at all the faces staring back at her, summing her up. If this wasn't the lion's den then she didn't know what was.

"We were just taking about how important this exchange will be for both of our institutions," Eric said. "During these very difficult economic times the arts are the first to be cut and we have to be creative. Even some of our biggest benefactors can't be as generous as they once were."

Zoe walked to an empty seat and sat down. She folded her hands on top of the table.

"Coffee?" Eric offered.

"No. Thank you, I'm fine. I'd really like to get an understanding about what is going on and why I'm being told I'm going to New York." She dropped her inquiring gaze onto one face after the other.

Eric chuckled. "You're being overly dramatic."

Zoe arched a brow. "Am I?"

"Why don't I explain?" interrupted Paul Shubert from the Guggenheim.

"Yes, please, explain," Zoe said, hoping she didn't sound quite as snappish as she thought she did.

He cleared his throat. "You see, the Guggenheim is in possession of the Thannhauser collection."

"Yes, part of your permanent collection," Zoe said. "Picassos, French Impressionists…"

"Yes, exactly. Recently we lost our curator for our African Art division. And the assistant is on maternity leave." He stole a look at Eric who indicated that he should go on. "The Guggenheim is much more known for its classic art. But over the years we have been working to expand our collections in each of the divisions. Now, however, with the cuts in funding any additions are nearly impossible."

"That's where you come in, Ms. Beaumont," Eric continued. "We want you to bring the same notoriety in the African Art division in New York as you did here with this most recent exhibit. It was a major coup for you to get the fertility statues here from the Ripley. And the exhibit has been a phenomenal success."

"It would only be for three months," Paul added.

"I know how much you are invested in your work and how dedicated you are to seeing the arts flourish," Eric said. "It would be beneficial to everyone concerned."

This was an opportunity of a lifetime. She knew that. She would have the chance to make her mark in New York. But why now?

"What about my job here?"

"You've trained Mike Williams well. He can take over until you return."

She sighed heavily. "Seems that it's been all figured out."

"I would think you'd be excited, Ms. Beaumont," Eric said.

"It's just a lot to take in."

"We'll need an answer soon."

She nodded. "What if I say no?"

"We hope that you won't," Eric said, his tone shifting from cajoling to edgy.

"I see. Let me talk it over with my family and the staff." She stood. "I'll have an answer for you tomorrow." She made eye contact with all the men in the room then walked out.

Her thoughts were spinning a mile a minute as she walked back to her office. Part of the offer sounded like a dream come true, but the other part sounded like an ultimatum. What would happen if she said no? A better question was why was she even thinking about not jumping on the next plane to New York? *Jackson Treme.*

When she sat down at her desk, her message light was flashing. Two messages were from Sharlene wanting to know how the meeting went. The other was from Jackson.

He was concerned about her and asked that she call when she got a break in her day. He only had one class and then office hours. After that he was heading home.

She replayed his message just to hear his voice. Her life was changing rapidly and she was trying her best to keep up. There was a knock on her door.

"Yes. Come in."

Linda stepped in. "Hi, there's a Michelle Treme here to see you."

A slight frown curled her brow. Michelle, what was she doing here? "Oh, okay. Show her back here."

"Sure."

Zoe paced the floor, her thoughts shifting back and forth between the meeting she'd just had, the decision she needed to make and what was happening between her and Jackson. She didn't think she could handle another complication—at least not before lunchtime.

Michelle poked her head in the door. "Hi."

"Come in." Zoe smiled and stepped around from behind her desk. "This is a surprise. Is everything okay?"

"Yes, and I'm sorry. I should have called first."

Michelle looked around the small office and Zoe thought she appeared a bit nervous.

"Don't worry about it. Have a seat. What's up?"

Michelle sat and rested her purse on her lap. "I was thinking about what you said the other night about possibly working here part-time." She fidgeted with the strap on her purse. "I was hoping that the offer was still open."

Zoe released the breath she held. This she could handle.

"Actually, yes, it is. Are you interested? I mean, you're planning to stay in Atlanta?"

"There's nothing for me back in New Orleans. I've thought about it and I need to start over. I talked it over with Jackson and he said we could stay as long as it took for me to get back on my feet. I contacted Shay's school in New Orleans and let them know she's not coming back. Unfortunately, the kindergarten classes in the area were all full but I got Shay set up in day care near the house. She'll be in first grade in September. Hopefully, I'll have my own place by then. But in the meantime, I know I'll go crazy in that house by myself all day."

Zoe's heart ached for her. She couldn't imagine what she was going through. She came and sat on the edge of her desk. She reached out and took Michelle's hand.

"First of all, I don't want you to think that this is some kind of a favor. We can use the help. It doesn't pay much, but it pays regularly. I'll expect you to work just as hard as everyone else. The position is only three days a week, though."

"That's fine."

"I have a few things to take care of, but I'll walk you over to Human Resources and you can fill out the application then we'll take it from there."

Michelle smiled with relief. "Thank you."

"Don't thank me yet. See how you feel after seven hours on your feet, answering an array of questions from patrons that have nothing to do with the tour *or* the museum!"

After Zoe took Michelle to Human Resources she came back to return Sharlene's phone calls.

"Zee, that is so fabulous for you."

"I know. I know," she agreed, leaning back in her office chair.

"I hear the hesitation. Why?"

"Let me start this way. When was the last time you've known me to make moves in my life based on someone else?"

"I'm going to press the 'easy button.' Never."

"Exactly."

"Well don't leave me hanging, girl. It's about Jackson, isn't it? Did he finally defrost your cold, cruel heart?" she teased.

"Very funny! This is serious, Sharl. I've never been in this place before."

"I know, sis. And it's probably scaring the heck out of you."

"And the dreams…"

"Worse?"

"More, almost every night now. And when I'm with Jackson…when we… It's crazy. I don't even know how to explain what happens. It's like I'm someplace else, someone else." She shook her head. "Hang on. Yes, come in," she called out.

Michelle poked her head in. "Hi. All done."

"Sharl, I'll call you back." She hung up the phone. "How'd it go?"

"Good. I have to bring in some documents, and then I'll get my start date."

"Great."

"Unfortunately, my papers are at the house in New Orleans."

"Jackson mentioned that he was planning to go down there next weekend," she said, and that uneasy feeling welled up in her stomach again.

"We didn't bring much when we left." Her gaze shifted away.

"Hey, if you're not busy, why don't you join me for lunch? I usually meet my friend Sharlene around one. You're welcome to come."

"Are you sure?"

"Of course."

She beamed. "Thanks. I don't have to pick Shay up until five. That's the one good thing about day care versus public school."

"Perfect." She checked her watch. "We have about an hour. If you want to hang out here, take a tour while I finish up some paperwork, then I'll meet you out front at about ten minutes to one and we'll walk over to Sharlene's office."

"Sounds fine." She draped the strap of her purse over her shoulder. She started for the door then turned toward Zoe. "Thank you. This all really means more to me than I can explain."

Zoe grinned. "Like I said, don't thank me yet. See you in a few."

"Wow, this place is fantastic," Michelle enthused as she walked around the Moore Design showroom.

The showroom housed everything from antique picture frames to exotic fabrics, one of a kind bowls and decorative objects, art deco wall art, and floral arrangements. It was a one-stop design shop for every taste and style.

"Sharlene has a fabulous eye for design and

finding the perfect pieces for her clients. She designed my town house."

"Really? When I get settled into my own place I will definitely be shopping here."

"And the prices are reasonable," Zoe added in a whisper.

"Hey, ladies," Sharlene greeted, breezing into the room.

"Sharlene Moore this is Michelle Treme, Jackson's sister."

Sharlene stuck out her hand. "Pleasure to meet you."

"Michelle is going to be working part-time at the museum."

"Wonderful. Great place and a wonderful staff. Zoe runs a pretty tight ship," she joked.

"I'm looking forward to it. But I have to tell you, this showroom is incredible. I don't know where to look first."

"Thanks. We try really hard to stock unique pieces. Customers want to know that their place isn't going to look just like someone else's."

"I was just telling Zoe that when I get my place, I'll be looking here first."

"Just let me know, and I'll hook you up. You ladies ready to go?"

"Yep," they chorused.

Jackson pulled into his driveway and got out. He still hadn't heard from Zoe. He didn't understand what had happened. They'd spent yet another fantastic night together but the morning brought an entirely different person. She could barely look at him and he had no idea why.

On top of that, he'd had a very disturbing conversation with the dean. The dean had received an anonymous letter from a female student alluding to sexual harassment on Jackson's part.

"Sexual harassment! You've got to be kidding me."

The dean handed him the letter he'd received.

Jackson read the short typed message in disbelief. He was stunned. The letter didn't give any specifics and it almost read like some kind of schoolyard prank.

"I haven't shared this with the administration as of yet. This is something that the administration takes very seriously, Professor Treme. Once it's turned over to them they will begin an immediate investigation."

Jackson felt like he was in some sort of alternate universe. This couldn't be happening.

"For the time being I'll hold on to this. You'll still be allowed to teach, since the alleged accuser wouldn't identify herself nor specify exactly what had taken place." He paused a moment and folded his hands on top of his desk. "I have to ask you this, professor." He looked Jackson squarely in the eye. "Could this be the reason why your teaching assistant, Victoria, left so abruptly?"

"No, absolutely not! This is crazy. She said it was purely personal and I took it at that."

The dean slowly nodded his head. "I see." He extended his hand for Jackson to return the letter. "Well, in the interim I would be mindful of being alone with any of your female students or giving off the impression that you favor one over the other. This could merely be a disgruntled student that you'd given a bad grade." He refolded the letter and put it in his desk drawer. "We'll revisit this in a few weeks. But I want to be clear, Professor Treme, I won't hesitate to bring this to administration if anything else should happen."

Jackson swallowed the dry knot in his throat and rose on stiff legs. "I understand. Thank you."

Numb, he'd walked out. Maybe he should have told him about Victoria's impromptu visit to his house and what she'd said. But instinct told him to keep that bit of information to himself. It may only have fueled the fire.

Jackson opened the front door and expected to find Michelle on the couch. The house was quiet. Any other day he would be concerned. But he was thankful for the solitude. He wanted to be alone for a while and think.

At least the semester would be over in a few weeks and he could step away from the whole mess. Hopefully, whoever had done this would be satisfied with nearly ruining his career and find someone else's to screw with.

He opened the fridge and took out a bottle of beer. He rarely drank at this time of the day, but under the circumstances he was making an exception.

Walking into the living room he stretched out on the couch, reached for the remote and turned on the television.

Every news channel was covering the latest uprising in the Middle East, the weather and the struggling economy. Turmoil had the upper hand no matter where you looked, he thought. Now it had invaded his private life as well.

He checked his cell phone. No missed calls or messages from Zoe. He tossed the phone across the table. It was just as well. He was up to his eyeballs in drama for the moment. And whatever it was that was bugging Zoe. Well, he wasn't in the frame of mind to deal with it now.

Chapter 19

"Oh, come on. I'm sure Jackson would be happy to see you. And you can stay for dinner. It's the least I can do to say thanks."

Michelle had no idea what had transpired between her and Jackson earlier, Zoe thought. She was probably the last person Jackson wanted to see and she had no one to blame but herself.

"Michelle, really, you don't have to do that."

Michelle clasped Zoe's arm. "I won't take no for an answer. I'm going to pick up Shay from day care and get dinner started. Come by about seven. I promise we'll make it an early night."

She looked at Zoe with puppy-dog eyes and Zoe couldn't say no.

"Okay. I'll come. But I want to bring something or at least help cook."

"Absolutely not. Just bring yourself and your appetite."

Zoe pushed out a breath. "Okay. See you at seven."

"Great." She leaned forward and kissed her cheek. "See you later."

Zoe walked back to her office. She hadn't even called Jackson back and she'd acted awful to him that morning with no explanation. He deserved one. And maybe Michelle's invitation was the opening that she needed to make things right.

In the meantime, she had calls to make and she needed to finish working on a grant to the National Endowment of the Arts that was taking a lot longer than usual. The chairman was right about one thing, funding was strained all over and the requirements for grants even more stringent. She needed to ensure that they got every dollar available.

He was also right about her love of what she did and her commitment to the arts. For as long as she could remember, art, artifacts and uncovering new treasures had been her passion. It was one of the things that made her and Sharlene so close over the years. They had the same artistic sensibilities. Sharlene chose to share her passion and love on a smaller scale. Zoe on the other hand wanted the world to enjoy what she loved.

She turned her computer on and loaded the application and began filling in the details from her notes and the data on the current budget.

"Hey, Zoe."

She looked up from the forms on her desk. "Hi, Mike. What's up?"

Mike walked halfway in. "I wanted to go over the shipment today. Thought you'd want to see it."

"Sure. I'll come down." She rotated the stiffness out of her neck then checked her watch. Wow. She'd been at it for nearly three hours straight, she realized. No wonder her body felt like a pretzel. She definitely needed a break. She got up and walked alongside Mike down to the storage room.

"I, uh, noticed that you were in with some of the board members this morning. Everything cool?" He angled a glance at her.

Zoe looked straight ahead. "Yes, some budget stuff."

"Are we okay?"

"Yes. I'm still working on the grant. But we should be good. We might have to cut back on some of the inventory and get a little more creative."

They took the stairs down two levels to the storage area.

"The new pieces are in that corner," Mike said, pointing to a stack of opened crates on the far side of the room.

Zoe took Mike's clipboard with the list of inventory that had been shipped from Tanzania and compared it to the merchandise in the crates. There were three glorious paintings of the Serengeti that were breathtaking.

The Serengeti was home to the largest mammal migration in the world and deemed one of the ten natural wonders of the world. Zoe had lobbied for months to get these pieces and it was worth it.

"Magnificent," she said, struck by the intricate detail of the riverine forests, swamps, the kopjes, grasslands and woodlands, blue wildebeests, gazelles, zebras and buffalos.

She spun toward Mike and instinctively hugged him, overcome with pure delight.

Mike wrapped his arms around her waist, lifted her off her feet and spun her around. "I kinda knew you would like it," he said, setting her down.

Zoe giggled with happiness. "These are going to look so awesome in the main corridor."

"That's what I was thinking."

She continued studying the paintings then she turned to Mike. "There is something else," she said, her tone sobering.

Mike's brows drew together. "What is it?" He tossed a tarp over the crates.

They started back out.

"I might be leaving for a few months. I haven't decided yet," she quickly added.

"Leaving? Why? What happened? I know the board can't be asking you to leave, not after the way you've turned this department around," he said, his ire rising.

"Come back to my office and I'll explain."

Mike sat with his ankle braced on his knee while Zoe explained the plan.

"So, I need to give them my answer sooner rather than later," she concluded.

He was quiet for a moment. "It's a phenomenal opportunity for you, Zoe."

She nodded in agreement. "I know."

"So why the hesitation?"

She glanced away. "It's personal. There's a lot going on in my life right now. I'm just not certain that this is the right time to pull up stakes. But on the other hand it would be beneficial to both museums."

"I'm sure you'll make the right decision. And I have your back whichever way you decide to go."

"It will be a major break for you, too, Mike. You get to run this division by yourself."

"You taught me well. And if given the chance I can handle it."

"I know you can. Well, I'll keep you posted."

He unwound his long muscular body and stood.

"Oh, and we're going to be getting a new part-timer, probably early next week. She'll be doing the tours and hopefully the genealogy classes."

"Cool."

"And Mike…"

"Yeah…"

"Thanks."

"For what?"

She smiled. "Just thanks."

He grinned. "See you later."

Zoe heaved a sigh and settled back in her chair. Now to tell Jackson.

Zoe pulled into the driveway of Jackson's house. She was more nervous now than the first night that they'd met. Even after she'd turned off the car she sat there, trying to get her thoughts and energy in order.

Before she had a chance to get out, the front door to Jackson's house swung open and Shay came running to the car.

"Miss Zoe," Shay called out, jumping up and down outside of Zoe's car window.

Her enthusiasm was contagious and Zoe immediately felt better. She grabbed her purse from the passenger seat and got out.

"Hey, sweetie. What a great welcome." She took Shay's hand and walked to the house. "I heard you started a new school today. Do you like it?"

"Yes, and my best friend's name is Missy!"

Zoe's eyes widened in delight. "Really? A best friend already?" She bit back a laugh.

"She said I'm her best friend, too."

"Of course."

Michelle greeted them at the door. "Hey. Right on time. Come on in."

Zoe's heart began to pound. She walked in and didn't see Jackson and tried not to think about what that meant one way or the other.

"Dinner is just about finished. Hope you like steak. Jackson insisted on helping. He's out back on the grill."

Her heart raced even faster and her stomach began to do figure eights.

"Why don't you go on out back? There's a pitcher of homemade iced tea on the table unless you want something stronger."

"No, um, iced tea is fine. Don't you need some help in here?" she asked, suddenly afraid of facing Jackson.

"Nope. Go on," she said softly, lifting her head toward the back door. Woman's instinct illuminated her expression. "It'll be fine."

Zoe didn't know whether to feel relief or embarrassed that Jackson may have told his sister how she'd behaved earlier. Either way, she couldn't stand in the kitchen like a lump forever.

"I want to come," Shay said.

"I need your help in the kitchen finishing up dinner. Can you help me like a big girl? And Miss Zoe can help Uncle Jack."

Shay looked from one grown-up face to the next. "I'll help you, Mommy."

"Why, thank you," she said to Shay and then winked at Zoe.

Zoe put one foot in front of the other and went out back. Jackson had his back turned to her while he worked the grill, and with his headphones plugged in he didn't hear her come up behind him. She tapped him lightly on the shoulder.

He turned halfway and his face seemed to light up from within. He pulled the buds out of his ears.

"Hey," he said softly.

Zoe felt her insides swell. "Hey."

"Glad you came."

"Me, too."

He reached out and cupped her cheek. For a moment he simply looked into her eyes and that said it all.

She leaned up and tenderly touched her lips to his. A sensation of completeness filled her. This was so very right, she thought as she felt his arm move around her waist and ease her closer to him. Her lips parted to accept the sweetness of his tongue in her mouth, and tiny bursts of electricity popped in her veins.

Her arms found their way around his neck as the kiss deepened taking on a life of its own. She sighed softly against his mouth.

"I'm sorry," she murmured.

He kissed her cheek then the tip of her nose. "I know." He stepped back without releasing her and took her in. "How good are you with the grill?"

"I can handle myself."

"I know that, too," he said with a teasing smile. He passed her an apron. "But let's see your grilling skills."

She swatted his arm and tied the apron around her waist and the friction between them from earlier was no longer a wall between them anymore.

Dinner was a lively affair with Shay being the center of attention regaling them with every minute detail of her first day in school. In between Michelle talked about how excited she was to be starting her new job and Jackson and Zoe couldn't wait to be alone.

Finally, Michelle announced that it was time for Shay to get ready for bed and excused them both for the night.

"I'll help you clean up," Zoe said, and began gathering plates and cups while Jackson made sure that the grill was off. They finished up and wandered into the living room.

"Can I get you anything?" Jackson asked.

"No. I'm good." She sat down on the couch and curled comfortably in the corner.

Jackson joined her. He put her feet on his lap and began to massage them.

"Hmm, that feels fabulous," she sighed.

"Easy tension reliever," he said, kneading the balls of her feet with deep strokes of his strong fingers.

Zoe closed her eyes and let the sensations take over. "I should have told you what was going on," she said, her voice almost dreamy.

"You're here now. If you want to talk about it, whatever it is, I'm listening."

She opened her eyes and looked at him. "The museum's board of directors wants me to go to New York…"

She told him how she was first approached and that the actual meeting was that morning, which was why she was so tense.

"Well, it wasn't the only reason," she confessed.

"What other reason, then?"

She swallowed. "You."

He momentarily stopped massaging her feet. "Me? Why me?"

She sat up and swung her feet to the floor. She pressed her palms to her thighs then turned to him. "Before I met you all there was in my life was my work. And then you came along like a whirlwind and nothing was the same. Something inexplicable is happening between us Jackson. It's scary and exciting and if I leave now, I, we, won't have time to see how this is going to work. *If* it's going to work out. I've never felt this way before and I…"

"Listen, no one knows better than me how important what we do is." He scooted closer to her. "Look at me."

She raised her head.

"There is no way in hell that I could live with

myself if I was the reason you didn't take this opportunity and run with it. I'm not going to hear it. You'll go to New York, kick some ass and come back."

"I'll be gone for three months."

"Would it be cool if you had company?"

"Company?"

A slow grin moved across his mouth. "School is out in three weeks. I'm off for the summer. What if I came with you to New York?"

She jerked forward. "What!" She leaped onto his lap. "Seriously?"

He laughed deep in his belly. "Yes, seriously. It's been ages since I've been to New York. You can do your thing during the day and we can paint the town at night and be back in time for your birthday."

She was jumpy all over with excitement. *Her and Jackson in New York. Together.* "Yes, yes, yes." She lathered his face with kisses.

"Come home with me," she said as they curled around each other on the couch, watching an episode of *Criminal Minds.*

"You sure, because I can tell you right now, you won't get much sleep."

"That's the whole idea, silly." She stretched up to kiss him.

"What if…" He raised his head to listen for movement from upstairs. "What if I gave you a little sample of what I was thinking about since you walked in the door?"

"Here? But what about—"

"They're asleep. And if you're a good girl and be quiet, they'll never know," he whispered deep in her ear while he stroked her thigh.

Zoe shifted her body so that she was beneath him. "Only if you promise not to do those things that make me noisy," she said, sucking in a breath when Jackson nibbled her neck.

"I hate to make promises that I can't keep." He reached up and turned out the lamp on the end table.

Zoe unbuttoned her blouse and tugged it out of the waistband of her skirt.

Jackson didn't waste a minute. He pushed her skirt up above her hips, unzipped his jeans then pushed her thong aside and entered her in one hard swift motion, covering her mouth with his to muffle her cry.

Zoe fumbled with the small pillow behind her head and managed to get it under her hips.

"Ohhh, baby," he groaned, dropping down into her deep well of wet, enveloping heat. A shudder ran up his back then down the inside of his thighs. Her gripped her hips and thrust long and strong. He felt her inner muscles squeeze him and he thought he'd lose his mind. His body had control now. He couldn't think. It was all crazy sensation and he was loving it.

"Right there, baby," she breathed in his ear

rotating her pelvis in a slow three-sixty taking every inch of him. "Oh…my…God. Yesss!"

Her entire body was on fire from the inside out. She bucked harder against him. She was so close. She felt it thumping, building deep in the pit of her stomach, tightening…and then he touched it, hit that spot and the lights in her mind flashed off and on and a near-violent orgasm tore through her with such force that she was bathed in white hot light.

And Jackson's loving overflowed in gush after gush and finally doused the last of her burning embers.

Chapter 20

Jackson and Zoe walked along Peachtree Street after having come from seeing the latest Tyler Perry movie.

Zoe listened in stunned silence while Jackson told her what was going on at the college. He'd decided to tell her in the event that there was any fallout. He didn't want her blindsided by any allegations. And if they were going to have a real relationship he knew that they would have to be honest with each other.

After that night at his house when Zoe broke down and told him that he was the reason why she'd hesitated about going to New York, he felt more confident in opening up to her as she had done. He didn't want secrets between them and he wanted her to feel safe with telling him whatever was on her mind.

Zoe squeezed his hand while they walked. Her thoughts tried to keep pace with the stream of information. Why would someone do something like that?

"So what now? I mean are they going to try to find out who sent the letter?"

"For the time being, no."

She was thoughtful for a moment. "You're okay with that?"

"I'm not okay with any of it. It's a real ugly feeling to have that hanging over your head. But I also don't want this to go to the next level and blow out of control. If the dean is willing to let it go, then I'll go along with it."

"Do you think it was that woman, Victoria?"

"No." He shook his head. "What would be her point, especially if she was planning on leaving anyway?"

"True." She leaned her head on his shoulder. "I'm glad you told me."

He kissed the top of her head. "So am I."

They turned the corner to where Jackson had parked his car. "How did your staff take the news about you leaving in two weeks?"

She laughed lightly. "Once they got over the shock and understood that I was coming back, it was like a party. They're really happy for me."

"So am I. Do you realize how important this is? The Guggenheim is one of the premiere museums in the world. And they want you, baby."

She looked up and him and grinned, seeing the look of pride and happiness in his face.

"I know, I know," she said, feeling a little giddy after finally accepting what was happening to her and her career.

They reached Jackson's car and he opened the door for her.

"So much has happened so fast," she said thoughtfully, settling into her seat. "It's hard to take it all in sometimes."

Jackson stuck the key in the ignition and turned on the car. "You seem to be handling it well." He pulled out of the parking spot.

She wanted to tell him about the dreams, the increasing frequency, explain all the stories she'd been told and that it would all culminate on her thirtieth birthday. As much as she'd dismissed it all as old family lore, it was becoming clear to her that something was definitely happening to her and there didn't seem to be anything she could do to stop it. She knew that when they made love it was no ordinary lovemaking. Although they'd never put it all into words, they had shared that they felt *something* had happened. She wasn't ready yet. But soon.

"Do you have everything you need for tomorrow night?" Zoe asked.

"Yeah, I think so. Michelle has totally taken over the plans. And I can't thank you enough for getting her the job. She's like a new person, smiling all the time, actually happy."

"It was nothing. There was an opening and she was there at the right time. She's doing great and she fits right in."

"That's good to hear. Having something to do everyday that she enjoys is just what she needs. Did she tell you that this was the first job she's had since college?"

"She did. That's just so hard for me to wrap my mind around—giving up your identity, your sense of self and turn it all over to someone else." She slowly shook her head.

"I guess she thought she was going to have a marriage like our parents. My father took care of the finances and my mother took care of the family. It worked for them."

"I have no idea what it's like growing up with two parents, good, bad or otherwise. I don't even know my father." She played with the clasp on her purse.

Jackson cast a look toward her. "From what I can tell, your folks did a fabulous job raising you."

She gave him a tight smile. "Yeah," she said softly. "I didn't turn out too bad."

"I'm looking forward to meeting your friend

Sharlene," he said, getting the feeling that he needed to switch topics.

Zoe chuckled. "Let's just say that the feeling is mutual."

"Shay asleep?" Zoe asked as she picked up the tray of crab meat salad and took it out back.

"Finally." Michelle sighed. "I thought she was never going to sleep."

The doorbell rang.

"That might be Sharlene. I'll get it." Zoe went to the door. "Hey, girl, right on time." She kissed Sharlene's cheek and took the small shopping bag from her.

"Zee, this is Ray. Ray, my best friend in the world, Zoe Beaumont."

"Nice to meet you. Come on in. We're just getting set up."

Sharlene and Ray walked inside.

"What did you bring? I told you that you didn't have to bring anything."

"What self-respecting Southern girl would come to a dinner party empty-handed?" She laughed, emphasizing her New Orleans twang. She leaned close and whispered in Zoe's ear. "Looks like you already have the run of the house, miss. You don't waste any time. Now where is Mr. Hot and Bothered?"

Zoe hugged her friend. "He's out back. Now act right," she warned. "Don't embarrass me."

"I'm offended."

"Right." She hooked her arm through Sharlene's and they joined Jackson and Michelle on the back deck.

Jackson was putting the beers in the cooler when they came through the door. Michelle was lighting citronella candles.

Zoe made the introductions to Michelle and Jackson.

"Good to finally meet you," Jackson said. "Zoe's been telling me all about you."

"Same here," Sharlene said with a grin and ignored the look that Zoe threw her way.

"Really?" He slid his arm around Zoe's waist. He kissed her forehead. He stuck his hand out to shake Ray's hand. "Can I get you a beer or something stronger?"

"Beer sounds good."

"Coming right up."

The front doorbell pinged in the distance. "Mikki, can you get that? It should be Levi."

"Sure. Ya'll help yourselves," she said before hurrying up front.

She got the door and pulled it open. Her breath caught. "Hi. You must be Levi."

His slow, easy smile greeted her. "And you must be Michelle."

"Yes."

They stood there caught in the split second of newness.

The sound of laughter coming from the group out back broke the spell.

Michelle stepped aside. "Please come in. Where are my manners?"

Levi walked past her. "Sounds like I'm late."

"No. We're just getting started."

He held up a bottle of wine, which Michelle took. "I'll put this on ice. Come. It's this way."

She led him through the kitchen and swore she felt his eyes on her every move. She opened the back door and stepped outside to the safety of the group.

"Hey man, 'bout time," Jackson greeted, giving Levi a half bear hug. "This is my buddy, Levi Fortune. A professor at Clarke-Atlanta and the recent recipient of his second doctorate," he announced with a flourish and held up a bottle of beer in salute.

The group applauded and followed with a flurry of congratulations and questions about his discipline and how he'd managed to teach and work on his dissertation at the same time.

Levi took it all in stride and in his quiet way answered the questions and then graciously turned the conversation away from himself and on current events.

The group filled their plates with salad, chicken kabobs, grilled shrimp and butter-soft steak. Music played in the background and the evening was warm and star-filled.

Michelle worked at keeping something in her hand or doing something other than stare at Levi.

She couldn't remember the last time she'd been so attracted to a man.

She'd been a married woman for ten years. And before Travis she could count the number of relationships she'd had on one hand. When she got married she'd turned off her radar, turned off her sex appeal to other men and ignored it when she saw it in them. Until now.

"What do you think, Michelle?" Jackson was asking.

She blinked and put down the glass she'd been holding. "Oh, I'm sorry, what were you saying?"

Jackson looked at her curiously. "I was asking what you thought about the genealogy program that you work on at the museum? Levi has been thinking about tracing his roots."

She shot a glance in Levi's direction and he was staring right back at her. She swallowed. "Well, I'm just getting the hang of it, but it's really fantastic, easy to learn. The patrons that come in to use it get a lot from it."

"Maybe I'll stop by one day and you can show it to me."

"Um, sure. Anytime. Well, Mondays, Wednesdays and Fridays."

"I'll keep that in mind."

"There's plenty more food," Zoe said, tickled at the energy popping back and forth between Michelle and Levi. "Can I refill any plates?"

"I'm stuffed," Sharlene said. "Everything was

wonderful." Ray took her hand. "We had a great time, but we're going to be heading out."

"Thanks for coming," Jackson said, standing to shake Ray's hand. "And it was good to finally meet you, Sharlene."

"We'll have to do this again. Maybe at my place next time," Sharlene said, gathering her things.

"I'll walk you out." Zoe excused herself and went with them to the door.

"I'll call you, sis," Sharlene said, then whispered in her ear, "Jackson is a hottie. You hit pay dirt this time."

"Don't I know it." She waved to Ray. "Take care of my girl."

"I plan to. Good night."

Zoe closed the door and returned to the deck. Jackson was reclining on a lounge chair and Michelle and Levi were in a quiet conversation. She eased up alongside Jackson.

"Hey, baby," she whispered. "Why don't we go inside and give them some space?"

He glanced over in his sister's direction then back at Zoe. He grinned and pulled himself up from the chair. "Come on, I'm sure we can find something to do."

Michelle didn't even notice that they'd left. She was totally absorbed in what Levi was saying.

He was funny, smart and good to look at, Michelle thought as he talked about his students and his love of teaching.

"What about you? Jackson told me a little but I'm sure not the important things."

"What would you like to know?"

"Tell me what you like to do when you're not being a mom, a sister, a great cook."

The question halted her for a moment. When she thought about it, that's all she was, all she had been for so long, she didn't know how to be anything else.

"I…I don't know really. That must sound silly. But…"

"No. It doesn't. But how about this. Since you're new in town and don't know your way around or what you like, what if…I showed you. Dinner, dancing, a movie."

"I…" She didn't know where to look. "I'm married. I mean…I couldn't."

"I'm sorry. That was out of line. I just thought… I'm sorry." He looked at her for a moment. "Hey, it's getting late, I should probably get going, too." He got up and Michelle's gaze rose with him.

"I don't know what Jackson may have told you about why I'm here."

"Nothing, really."

"I just left a bad relationship. I didn't know it was bad at the time. But…anyway, it's too soon for me to be thinking about—"

"Getting involved. Look I totally understand. I only thought that if you wanted to do something sometime, I'd be willing. When you're ready—to be a friend."

She bobbed her head.

"So, maybe I can stop by the museum, on a Monday, Wednesday or a Friday and if you're not busy," he said with a soft smile on his lips, "you might want to have lunch…or something."

"Okay. I'd like that."

"Good." He leaned down and lightly kissed her cheek. "Good night, Michelle."

"Good night."

Michelle rested back against the seat, listened to the door open and close. Her heart was still beating a mile a minute.

A man, a handsome, intelligent man had asked her out. She didn't know how to be with anyone other than Travis. She looked toward the door. But she was willing to learn all over again. And maybe Levi would be the one to teach her.

Chapter 21

"We're heading out," Jackson said, walking into the kitchen.

Michelle turned from the sink. "I should go with you."

"No, you shouldn't. It's a seven-hour ride going and coming. You told me what you need me to pick up, I'm going to do it and that's it. I don't want you going back there." He walked up to her. "Look at me. It's best this way."

She blinked back impending tears. "You're right. I know that." She lowered her head.

"I'll be back late tonight. Me and Levi are going to take turns driving. So don't worry."

"Okay," she managed. "Just be careful."

"You know he likes you, don't you."

Her face heated. "Did he say that?"

"He didn't have to, he asks about you enough. Maybe when all of this mess is over…" He lightly shrugged his shoulder.

"We'll see."

He kissed her cheek. "Later." He turned to leave.

"I like him, too," she called out.

"Yeah, I know," he tossed over his shoulder.

Michelle leaned against the sink and folded her arms. *He liked her.* It was a start.

Jackson pulled up in front of Levi's house and blew the horn. Levi had purchased the house in a foreclosure two years earlier. It needed extensive work when he bought it, but over time he'd turned it into a show piece. He'd gutted the whole house and room by room restored it, replacing the hardwood floors, the crown molding and fireplaces. He'd put in new windows and doors, a new bathroom and upgraded the kitchen. But he'd managed to keep the old charm about the house with some modern upgrades. Levi was definitely a renaissance man. He was smart *and* handy. If Levi did wind up with his sister, he wouldn't lose sleep over it.

"Hey, man," Levi greeted, hopping into the passenger seat. He handed Jackson a travel mug of hot coffee. "For the road."

"Thanks." He placed the mug in the cup holder

and put the car in gear. "I figure we try to drive straight through. Get what we need to get and come right on back."

"Fine with me. Just let me know when you want me to drive."

Jackson turned on the radio.

"So what kind of guy is this Travis?"

"If you would have asked me that six months ago I would have told you he was a great guy, hard worker, good husband and father." He jaw clenched. "That was six months ago."

"I don't understand guys like that. If you're unhappy then get the hell out."

"Yeah," Jackson grumbled.

"And with your ex?" He shook his head in amazement. "Takes all kinds of people."

They were quiet for a while. "Hey, listen, man, you think if I asked Michelle to go out with me, she would? Or you think it's too soon? Hey, maybe it's not even cool with you about me asking about your sister." He reached for his mug of coffee and took a long swallow.

Jackson looked at him out of the corner of his eye. "It's cool with me and I think she might say yes."

Levi grinned like he'd won money. "Awright. That's a good thing." He bobbed his shaved head in time to his words.

"Just remember, she's my sister so I don't

want to hear anything I shouldn't be hearing. You feel me?"

"Yeah, yeah, man. I hear ya." He settled back to enjoy the ride.

Zoe's head was pounding. She'd awakened with a headache and couldn't seem to shake it off. It had been a while since she'd had such a whopper. They generally came after she'd had one of those dreams about running. And she'd wake up the next morning with a feeling of dread and a blinding headache.

All of her senses today were surrounding Jackson. She couldn't put her finger on what it was. But she felt unsettled every time she thought of him. It was the first night since they'd been intimate with each other that they had not spent the night together. Perhaps that was it; simple separation anxiety.

She'd always pooh-poohed Nana when she told her that her heightened senses were a gift if she learned to use them. Zoe didn't want to hear it. She wanted to experience life in the same order as everyone else. She didn't want to know anything that she wasn't supposed to know. But today was different. She couldn't shake the tightness in her belly or the sensation that something was wrong. Heightened senses or not, she knew in her soul that it had to do with Jackson.

She tried to relax her mind and open it the way Nana always told her, become one with her surroundings. All she got for her troubles was the same pounding in her head. Maybe she should have listened all those years ago.

She picked up her coffee cup from the kitchen table and walked to the back window. The sky was gray, almost dingy. She could see the storm clouds brewing in the distance. Dropping the curtain back in place she wished that they'd chosen another day to drive to New Orleans.

Levi pulled out of the rest stop having switched places with Jackson for the balance of the ride.

"Making pretty good time," Jackson said, buckling up.

"I figure another two hours tops. Sky looks pretty ugly, though."

"Yeah, I was thinking the same thing. Hope we're not fighting the weather on the way back."

"So everything cool with the job? No more notes?"

"No. So far everything is quiet. And I want to keep it that way."

"I hear ya. Nothing worse than having those kinds of accusations thrown at you. Hard as hell to fight."

"Yeah, exactly. I still can't figure who would do something like that. For what purpose?"

"Obviously to mess with you, bro." He merged onto the exit ramp. "I gotta tell you though, I still think Victoria has something to do with it."

"Man, I thought the same thing, but it doesn't

make sense to go through all that trouble and then leave."

"Hey, maybe it was her last hurrah. Who knows, man, women can have all kinds of reasons for doing stuff that men will never understand."

Jackson snorted a laugh and leaned back.

Two hours later they pulled into the parish of St. Tammany, one of the most affluent parishes in New Orleans and the fastest growing. The stately homes were graced with towering willow trees and lush green, well-manicured lawns. There was a quiet elegance to the community.

"So this is where your sister lived," Levi commented, eyeing the homes.

"Yeah, ten years. A far cry from where we grew up."

"Where'd you grow up?"

"Ninth Ward. Great people, tight knit, but not well off. Most folks struggled the majority of their lives to make ends meet. Not always first in line for services from the government, either. But we survived. We were happy, though."

"How'd Michelle meet Travis?"

"Make your next right. It's on the next street." He paused a moment. "I introduced them," he said through tight lips. He shook his head in regret. "Biggest mistake I ever made, next to getting involved with Carla."

"Hey, you couldn't have known."

He turned and looked hard at his friend. "I don't intend to make that mistake again."

"Understood."

"Right there." Jackson pointed to a two-story brick house.

"Nice," Levi murmured, pulling into the long driveway. "Doesn't look like anyone's home." He cut the engine.

They got out and approached the front door. Jackson rang the bell as a courtesy before putting his sister's key in the lock.

The house was dark and quiet and smelled like a liquor still. Jackson flicked the light switch on the wall and the chaos was bathed in soft white light.

Empty bottles, take-out cartons, newspapers and dirty clothes were on every surface.

"What the hell happened in here?" Levi asked, stepping over a pile of papers.

"Maybe he had an attack of conscience. Come on," he said. "I want to get Michelle and Shay's things and get out of here." He led the way to the upstairs bedrooms, walked down the hall to the room that Michelle shared with Travis and opened the door. At first he didn't see him and then his gaze settled on the figure sitting still as stone in a chair by the window.

Jackson turned on the light and nothing happened.

"Light out?" Levi asked, not knowing what was going on.

"Looks like Travis is home after all." He stepped fully into the room that was in total disarray. He crossed the room and stood over the inert form of his brother-in-law. He roughly shook his shoulder.

Travis groaned, struggled to open his eyes and when he was finally able to focus he lurched back in the easy chair.

"What the hell are you doing in my house?" He wobbled to his feet, weaved for a moment before finding his footing.

"Save it, Travis. I came to get my sister's and my niece's things."

"Where's my wife and my daughter?"

"Your wife and your daughter! What the fuck do you care?" Jackson bellowed. "After what you did to her, to Shay…" He stepped closer and caught the stench of his unwashed body and days of drinking. For a hot minute he wondered what had happened to Travis, why he was living like this. But the moment quickly passed. He shoved him back down into the chair. "Stay out of my way until I'm done."

He whirled away and went to the closet, nearly ripping the door from its hinges and began taking what was left of Michelle's clothes out the closet. Michelle told him that all of her papers were in a metal lockbox in the back of the closet. He looked behind the shoe rack and found the box.

Jackson handed off the clothes to Levi who placed them in a big duffel bag that they'd brought along. He kept his eye on Travis while Jackson went through the dresser drawers taking whatever he thought Michelle might need. Jackson slammed the drawers shut rattling the mirror on top.

"Come on," he growled.

Jackson stormed out and went down the hall to Shay's room. He turned on the light and was stunned to see that it was pristine. All of Shay's toys and stuffed animals were neatly placed on shelves. Her bed was made and covered with a *Dora the Explorer* quilt. In the center of the room was a round pink table and two pink chairs.

Seeing it all, being in this house, the full impact of the life that his sister had led and was now destroyed by that no good bastard wallowing in the other room roared through him and exploded in his head.

"Damn it! I want to kill him." He paced the room, his blood pumping.

"Take it easy man." Levi grabbed Jackson's arm. "I know this is rough. Let's do what we came to do and get out of here."

Jackson's nostrils flared. He stomped over to the closet and started taking out Shay's clothes. They gathered as much of her toys as they could carry and put them in another duffle bag.

"I'm going to take this stuff out to the car," Levi said, while Jackson began taking the table apart.

"Yeah, I'll be done in a minute. I know Shay is going to want her table and chairs."

"Be right back."

Jackson was working on the last screw when Travis appeared in the doorway. In the light, he looked worse than Jackson thought.

"I want my wife back," he said, his voice raw and ragged.

"Ain't gonna happen."

"This isn't what I wanted."

Jackson jumped up from his spot on the floor. "Not what you wanted!" He strode toward him, calling on his willpower not to knock Travis into next week.

"She won't answer my calls. She won't let me talk to my baby. Just ask her to call me. I need to tell her that I'm sorry."

"Sorry. Sorry. It's not enough Travis. Sorry will never be enough for the pain you've caused." He got up on him, grabbed him by his collar. "Why? And with Carla. How could you?" He shoved him in the chest and turned back to getting the table unscrewed.

"It was all Carla," he said in a broken voice.

"Yeah, she put a gun to your head and told you to screw up your marriage." He picked up the parts from the table and tucked them under his arm, grabbed the quilt with his other hand and pushed by Travis in the doorway. "Get your mistress to clean this place up," he said on his way down the stairs.

"It was her plan all along. It was never about me," he said leaning over the railing of the staircase.

"That's what she told me after Michelle walked out on me."

Jackson stopped at the bottom of the landing and looked up.

"It was all about hurting you and anyone that you cared about. She wanted to get back at you! You!" He tossed his head back and laughed a heartrending laugh then crumbled into a heap.

Levi was coming back through the door and took in the scene. Jackson looked like someone had died. "Jack… Hey, man, what's going on?" His gaze rose up the staircase and for a minute he thought the worst until Travis pulled himself up and staggered back down the hallway.

"Let's go. We have a stop to make."

They packed up the backseat and storage area in the Explorer, just as the rain started coming down. Jackson got in behind the wheel and before Levi was barely in his seat, Jackson was tearing away from the curb.

"You want to tell me what happened back there?"

Jackson stared straight ahead. The blood was pounding in his temples. He whipped the car around the corner, drove another two streets down and screeched to a jerking stop.

Jackson's door flew open and he jumped out, storming toward a blue and white house. He took note of the fact that Carla's fire-engine red Altima was parked in the driveway. No other car in sight.

He bounded up the four steps and pounded on the door.

Moments later the door was pulled open. From where Levi was standing she was stunning, a good ringer for Vanessa Williams. He closed his door and waited by the car. He wasn't sure what was going on but he had a good feeling the woman in the doorway was Carla and this visit was personal.

"Jackson!" Her green eyes lit up from within." I knew you'd come back." She reached for him and he slapped her hand away.

"Why'd you do it, Carla?" His jaw tightened.

She jerked back.

"Huh, tell me why you did it. Tell me what Michelle ever did to you."

Her soft expression hardened. "She had everything, a beautiful home, a husband, a daughter. And I had nothing. Nothing when you left! We were planning a life together. Me and you, Jackson," she yelled, jamming a finger in her chest. Her skin flushed. "I wanted to have children with you!"

"It was over between us long before we made it official, Carla. You know that. Things hadn't been right for a while."

"It wasn't over for me." Tears filled her eyes. "Couldn't you see that?" She stepped toward him and he moved away.

"Is that when you started sleeping with Travis? Were you screwing my sister's husband when we were together?"

"No," she whimpered. "No. Not until after you left."

He snorted his disgust. "I guess that made it okay. I can't imagine how I could have cared about you. How I could have thought…" He pointed a finger at her. "Go to hell and take Travis with you." He spun away and ran down the steps.

"I hate you!"

Jackson was seeing red as he stomped back to his car. The rain was coming down heavier now but he barely noticed. Could she have been so twisted that she would use their breakup as a reason to destroy Michelle's marriage? What kind of woman was she and how could he have been so blind to have…

Levi stopped him before he got behind the wheel. "Let me drive."

Without a word, Jackson got into the passenger seat and they pulled off.

Zoe sat at the window watching the rain build in intensity. Thunder rumbled in the distance and periodic flashes of light illuminated the dull sky.

Her spirit felt as heavy as the clouds that hung like water balloons in the sky. She hadn't heard from Jackson since he'd called that morning to say that they were leaving. And her calls to him had gone directly to voice mail.

Hopefully, they were close and the trip hadn't done more damage than good. She leaned her head against the cushion of the chair and closed her eyes.

The distant ringing of her phone pierced her consciousness. She blinked against the darkness that had enveloped the room and went for the phone on the nightstand.

"Hello?"

"Hey, baby."

"Jackson! When did you get back?"

"About twenty minutes ago. We just finished unpacking the car."

"Are you all right?" She knew that he wasn't even as she asked.

"Feel like some company?"

"Always," she said.

"See you soon."

"She said she did it because of me, Zoe," he spoke quietly into the dimly lit bedroom. "I feel responsible."

Zoe squeezed his hand as they lay side by side in her bed. "There is no way you could have known. You can't blame yourself, Jack." She turned onto her side. His outline was framed by the moonlight. She caressed his cheek. "Everyone made choices. Now they have to live with them. Carla can blame you all she wants, but in the end the choice was hers alone. Hers and Travis's. The only person's actions you can be responsible for are your own. That's it."

He turned his head to look at her. "I get that but it doesn't stop the hurt, ya know?"

"I know, baby. I know." She rested her head on his chest.

Jackson leaned back a bit and lifted her chin. His dark gaze skimmed over her face that to him was growing more beautiful everyday. "I'm falling in love with you, Zoe." The words tumbled from his mouth like a prayer.

Zoe felt her heart jump. Her lips parted to speak, to tell him what had been born in her spirit but his mouth captured hers. And as she turned herself over to him she knew she heard the words echo in her soul, words that she didn't speak.

He knows.

Chapter 22

"What am I going to do without you for three whole months?" Sharlene asked as they walked along the racks of their favorite boutique, Parade.

Zoe wanted to pick up some clothes suitable for New York nightlife, so she and Sharlene met after work to do some much needed shopping.

"Stay busy and keep Ray busy. How is that going, anyway?"

"I really like him. Great guy. Easy going. Settled. Great in bed," she added with a wicked laugh. "And you're going to have Mr. Hot and Bothered all to yourself for three months. *And* they're putting you up in a condo. How lucky is that?"

Zoe bcamed inside. Since she'd met Jackson,

her life had been like a fairy tale come true. He awakened something in her that had been dormant. *Love.* And everything he touched in her life became golden. She felt alive when she was with him and ached when they were apart.

"You want me to drive you guys to the airport in the morning?"

"No. We're going to take a car service." She took a short black cocktail dress from the rack and held it up. "What do you think?"

"I think Jackson Treme has got a whole lotta trouble on his hands."

Zoe grinned. "I think I'll take it."

Zoe's stomach was a mass of butterflies as she packed her suitcase. This was a big step on a lot of levels, for her career and for her relationship with Jackson. She had the opportunity to make a real name for herself in the arts industry. If she was successful, the sky was the limit as to what she could do next. And for the next three months she and Jackson would actually be living together. Waking up and sleeping with each other, every day. What if it was a disaster? What if they realized that it was all a terrible mistake? What if he realized that he didn't love her after all?

She wouldn't go there. She wasn't going to sabotage everything with negative thinking. She pulled in a breath of resolve. She was going to be open, receptive, give in to her real feelings and see where it took her. But what frightened her most was that everything that her grandmother predicted was coming true. And if everything else was true...

She picked up a blouse, looked at it then tossed it aside in favor of another. She was sorting through her toiletries when the phone rang. Crossing to the other side of the bed, she sat down and picked up the cordless phone.

"Hello?"

"Hey, sweetheart."

"Ma. How are you?" She tucked the phone between her cheek and shoulder and returned to her packing.

"I wanted to wish you a safe flight."

"Thank you."

"All the plans are underway for your party. You will be back in time, won't you?"

"Yes, I'll be back the first week in August if everything goes right."

"It will," she said with meaning. "How are things going with your young man?"

"Fine. He's...coming with me to New York."

"Oh, for a visit?"

"No, he'll be staying with me while I'm there."

Silence hung on the line.

"Oh. Do you think that's wise?"

Zoe's neck jerked back. "Wise? What do you mean, do I think it's wise?"

"I mean is it appropriate for you to be staying with a man...who's not your husband?"

Zoe shook her head in shocked disbelief. "I don't mean any disrespect, Ma, but that's none of your business. And you're the last person who should have anything to say about appropriate behavior," she snapped. "You don't even know who my father is!"

The painful arrow of truth hit its mark and Zoe could feel it reverberate through the phone. She felt sick. No matter what kind of relationship she had with her mother, she'd never been disrespectful. No matter how much she'd disappointed her, failed on her promises. Zoe always remembered what Nana told her. *That's your mother. And you respect your mother.*

"I'm sorry. I shouldn't have said that."

"Yes…you should have. I owe you so much, Zoe. And I owe you the truth."

Zoe's heart began to thunder. She slowly sat down on the side of her bed.

"When you get back, when you come home… we'll talk. Okay? Will you give me that?"

Her throat was so tight she could barely get the word out. "Yes."

Jackson got out of the cab and helped Zoe to her feet. The driver got out and helped them take their bags out of the trunk. And much like typical tourists visiting New York, their eyes went skyward to the towering buildings that cut across the skyline.

"Gotta be impressed," Jackson commented, taking out his wallet to pay the driver.

"Yeah," Zoe said in awe, watching the yellow cabs fly down the busy streets, and the stylish pedestrians walking and talking on cell phones, oblivious to the swell of activity that would put most out-of-towners into overdrive.

The doorman of the full-service condominium met them at the curb with a cart to take their bags.

Jackson and Zoe looked at each other in wide-eyed amusement.

"I could get used to this," Jackson whispered in her ear as they followed the doorman inside.

"What floor?" He turned to ask them.

"Twenty," Zoe replied. "Twenty-two hundred."

"Yes, ma'am, the penthouse suite."

Zoe and Jackson snatched a glance at each other and mouthed "penthouse."

They followed the doorman to the bank of elevators and tried to contain their excitement. He stuck a special key in the panel and the doors swooshed shut.

Exiting on the twentieth floor the elevator opened directly onto the suite.

"Where would you like your bags, sir?"

Jackson was momentarily taken aback by the sheer luxury of the space. "Uh, you can leave them by the couch. Thank you." He dug in his jacket pocket for his wallet.

"That won't be necessary sir. It's all covered in

the HOA fees. You can pick up your elevator key at the front desk. And if there is anything you need, just pick up the white house phone."

"Thank you," Zoe was able to manage.

He dipped his head. "Enjoy your day."

The instant the elevator door closed behind him, Zoe and Jackson whooped in delight. He swept her up and spun her around in a circle.

"I can't believe this place," she said breathlessly. She walked across the open living space, the sound of her heels clicking across the gleaming hardwood floors that ran throughout the apartment. The window rose to the ceiling and looked out on the magnificent skyline of Manhattan. The kitchen opened onto the entertainment area and was totally high-end; stainless steel appliances, granite countertops and an L-shaped island.

The furnishings in the living room were straight out of HGTV's *Selling New York*. Now, Zoe knew her art and so did Jackson. The pieces that hung on the walls they both agreed were originals and so were the sculptures that sat atop the stone fireplace and the glass-and-chrome shelving unit.

"Let's see the rest," Zoe said, taking Jackson's hand and walking down a short hallway. Double doors opened onto the master suite.

"Oh, my goodness," Zoe breathed, stepping into a fairy tale.

The centerpiece was the king-size bed overflowing with pillows in a variety of sizes and a multitude of color on a brilliant white overstuffed comforter. To the side was small sitting nook and the entire opposite wall was a massive walk-in closet.

"What's through here?" Jackson walked to another set of doors that opened onto what was no less than a spa bathroom.

"Okay, I'm done," Zoe said looking around in wonder at the double sink, overhead cabinets, massive glass shower with a rain showerhead and then there was the Jacuzzi tub.

"This is unbelievable. Who lives here?" Jackson asked, testing out the high-end faucets.

"Chairman Lang said that it's leased to the museum for short and long-term guests." She peeked inside one of the cabinets to find row upon row of towels and milled soaps and shampoos.

Jackson wandered out of the bath and turned the corner to find another bedroom and a smaller but no less exquisite bathroom. The next door opened onto a fully-equipped home office.

Zoe caught up with him in the hallway. She propped her hand on her hip. "So, uh, what do you think of the accommodations?" she asked.

"I think we're going to have to flip for the Jacuzzi!"

She walked up to him and wrapped her arms around his waist. She looked into his eyes. "I'm happy you're here with me."

"So am I." He kissed her lightly.

"And I can't wait to check out that king-size bed."

* * *

Eager to explore the city during the day, they changed clothes, checked in with the front desk for the passkey for the elevator and ventured out.

The condo wasn't far from the museum, situated on East 88th Street and Madison Avenue. They walked over to Fifth Avenue, marveling at the shops along the famous avenue that they'd seen in magazines and on television and the amazing amount of people out shopping in the middle of a weekday. So much for a tight economy when it came to New Yorkers, Jackson had commented.

They found a little outdoor bistro and stopped for soup and sandwiches then they walked over to the Guggenheim.

"This is it," Zoe said as they stood outside the ornate doors.

Jackson draped his arm around her shoulder. "You're going to do a fantastic job," he said, sensing her trepidation.

"You think so?"

"I know it." He kissed her forehead. "Come on, let's get back to our lap of luxury and relax. You have a busy day tomorrow."

And it was. From the moment she walked through the door the following morning it was nonstop activity. She met with the staff, got a tour of the facility and was thrown directly into her new temporary job. She spent the better part of the day reviewing what pieces the museum currently had in house and going over the budget and what grants were outstanding. By the time her day was over she was totally exhausted and was thrilled to see Jackson waiting for her in the lobby.

She walked right up to him and kissed him fully on the lips. "I'm so glad to see you."

He put his arm around her and they walked out. "How did it go today?"

"Tiring and exciting. There's so much to do in a little bit of time."

"You can handle it. That's why they chose you and not someone else."

She leaned against him while they walked. "Yes, they did, didn't they." She looked up at him and smiled with a renewed confidence, feeling deep within that with Jackson in her corner, she could accomplish anything.

Chapter 23

Zoe's days were filled but she was making progress. She'd completed three new grants, which she was confident that the museum would receive, and she'd begun selecting new inventory, using many of her contacts and connections that she'd established over the years. Several of the shipments had arrived.

They'd been in New York for more than two months and she couldn't believe how quickly the time had passed. In a matter of weeks the new exhibit would be mounted and she would finally be able to go home.

Whatever trepidations she'd had about "living" with Jackson were gone. She looked forward to each day waking up with him and coming home to him at night. She'd even begun thinking about a real future with him.

As the weather in New York grew warmer, they visited many of the city's hot spots, from the Blue Note in the Village where they listened to live jazz, the Statue of Liberty and the Empire State building to boat rides on the Hudson at Chelsea Piers.

They found local restaurants that became their favorites and they'd become experts at ordering in from the innumerable restaurants that delivered.

And at night they found each other and made slow and passionate love that bound them even more closely together. The last thing she expected in their oasis of bliss was the proposition that had the potential to change everything.

She was in her small, cramped office going over the inventory list when she got a call from Eric Lang.

"Chairman Lang. How are you?"

"I'm well. And from what I've been hearing you have done a magnificent job."

"Thank you. What can I do for you?"

"I'm calling because I've been in discussions with the administration and the board at the Guggenheim."

She sat up straighter in her seat. "Yes." She put down her pen.

He cleared his throat. "The Board at the Guggenheim want to make you an offer."

"An offer. What kind of offer?"

"To oversee the collection in all the divisions."

The air stopped in her chest. "What?"

"They want someone with your expertise, not only in African American art but in funding streams as well, and your knowledge of the other divisions."

Zoe was stunned into silence.

"I know this is a big decision, Ms. Beaumont. I don't expect you to give me an answer right now. The Guggenheim Board is putting together an offer—a very substantial offer."

Her thoughts were on scramble. "What about my job at the High?"

"Mike is doing a wonderful job. He's taken on his new responsibilities and we are all very pleased. We have you to thank," he added as if that would somehow soften the blow.

"Are you saying that my job is gone?"

"Well…we are considering making some changes."

"Changes." She couldn't breathe. Her face felt hot.

"I do hope that you will think about this. An offer like this one should not be taken lightly. It's not been done before. You should feel immensely proud. We'll talk soon."

Zoe sat there, numb with the phone still in her hand until the buzzing dial tone snapped her back to her new reality.

Finally she hung up the phone, got her purse and checked out for the day. She didn't call Jackson.

He'd told her that morning that he was going to hang out in the village and maybe do some shopping for Michelle and Shay. They'd planned to meet back at the condo that evening.

Zoe strolled the streets of the city and found that the sights and sounds that had excited her when she'd arrived now assaulted her senses. The car horns were louder. The people seemed to have multiplied. The overabundance and excess of everything overwhelmed her.

She wandered into a small eatery and was shown a table in the back. For more than an hour she played with the burger she ordered and nursed a Diet Coke.

She'd built her career at the High. She'd turned it around. For nearly a dozen years, Atlanta had been home for her. And now...

She should be elated. It was true that this was an opportunity beyond anything she could have imagined. But how could she live in New York with a dream job and not have Jackson to come home to?

Her insides felt as if they were splitting. What was she going to do?

When she got back to the condo, Jackson was already there. She wasn't ready to talk to him about this and knowing him and what he wanted for her, he would tell her to go for it. And that's not what she wanted to hear.

"Hey, babe."

"Hey." She put on her best face and crossed the

room to where he was on the couch. She plopped down beside him and rested her head on his chest.

"Tired?"

"Yeah, a little."

"Well, another week and we'll be back home and hopefully you won't have to work so hard."

"Yeah." She drew in a long slow breath. "I'm going to take a shower."

"I fixed dinner. Thought we could stay in tonight. Relax."

"Sure."

He watched her walk away, and as much as she'd tried to hide it he saw the trouble in her eyes. She'd talk when she was ready. She always did. He'd give her the space to do that.

In the months that they'd been together he grew to understand the nuances that made Zoe Beaumont so incredible. She was a confluence of complexity, but she was loving and caring and passionate about her work and her family. She was funny and smart and carried the scars of her past deep inside. He hoped with time that he could help her heal some of them. If she would let him.

Zoe stared into the darkness, unable to sleep. Her thoughts wouldn't stay still. She wanted to talk with Jackson about what had happened, that if she went back to Atlanta, she wouldn't have a job and if she stayed in New York she would have the job of a lifetime.

At first coming to New York had been an obstacle because of Jackson. But when she'd finally told him, he'd made it all okay and here they were—together. But how could he make this okay? Would he pick up and come to New York, leave his job, his career? She couldn't ask him to do that. She wouldn't.

Their last week in New York was a flurry of activity for Zoe. The show was mounted, the brochures printed, the opening scheduled and the offer on her desk.

They wanted her decision, preferably before she returned to Atlanta. She hadn't decided what she was going to do but what she had decided was that she was going home, celebrate her birthday with her family, talk with her grandmother and find out what her mother had been hiding from her for thirty years.

Chapter 24

"One of the best getaways I've had," Jackson said as he walked with Zoe to her door.

"Me, too. I'm glad you came with me. Really." She dug inside of her purse for her key.

"Me, too," he said before stealing a quick kiss.

She opened the door and Jackson brought her bags inside.

Zoe turned on the lights and looked around, realizing with a pang just how much she'd missed her house. "It's good to be back," she said on a breath.

"And as much as I'd love to rechristen your bedroom I need to get going. The meter is running on the cab."

She walked up to him and scooped her arms around his waist. "Thank you."

"For what?" He looked down into her eyes, hoping to find the answers that were just out of reach.

"For being you. For being wonderful. For putting up with me. I know I haven't been easy these past couple of weeks. It's just been—"

"Hey," he said gently, cupping her chin. "I love you. Don't you believe that by now? And I'm there for you." He pulled her close and held her, feeling her heart pound against his chest.

The cab driver honked the horn.

"You'd better go before he makes off with your bags for payment."

"I'll call you in the morning. Get some rest."

She nodded, walked with him to the door and slowly closed it behind him.

Sharlene set her glass down on the coffee table in Zoe's living room. "What do you mean you don't have a job?"

"I either take the job in New York or I'm unemployed."

"Can they do that?"

"Apparently." She curled her legs beneath her on the couch.

"I don't get it. They gave you no indication that helping them out in New York was going to lead to this. So what are you going to do?"

"I don't know. That's what I've been battling with for the past couple of weeks."

"Have you talked it over with Jackson?"

"No."

"Why not, Zoe? Maybe he could help you figure it out."

"He can't help me and I already know what he's going to say."

"What is he going to say?"

She sighed. "He's going to tell me to take it. He's going to tell me that it's the chance of a lifetime. I'd be the first African American woman in that position. He'd tell me all of that."

"And…"

"It's not what I want to hear."

"Well, what do you expect him to say, Zoe? 'Give up your career and stay here with me, baby, I'll take care of you'?"

"Yes! I mean, no. I don't know what I mean."

"Zoe, give the man a chance. Be honest with him. Who knows, he may want to come to New York, teach at one of the colleges there. You won't know if you don't talk to him."

"I wouldn't do that to him. I wouldn't put him in that kind of position."

"So what are you going to do then? Pretend to go to work every day? How long do you think you can pull that off?"

She pressed her fist to her mouth. "I'm going to take the job in New York."

Sharlene jerked back in surprise. "You are?"

"What choice do I have? It's what I do. It's what I know."

"And you can't hide behind your job forever." She got up from the couch. "He deserves to know how you feel."

Zoe looked up at her friend.

"Tell the man how you feel. Tell him what's in that heart of yours. For once. Say what's in your heart." She walked barefoot toward the kitchen. "I think you'll be surprised."

She rested her head against the back of the couch and closed her eyes. *There will come a time when you will have to make a choice.* She heard her Nana's words ring in her head.

But which choice should I make Nana? Which choice should I make?

"Ready?" Sharlene asked.

Zoe opened her eyes.

Sharlene had her purse in her hand and her sunglasses on. "Come on, girl, we have some birthday shopping to do. You're going to be the big 3-0 in less than a week. You have to be sharp."

Zoe pulled herself up.

"Shopping always soothes my soul," she said, giving her a quick squeeze. "Put your shoes on and let's go."

"All right, all right. But I have plenty of clothes in my closet that I can wear."

"Nothing suitable for your big day. And I think it's going to be really special."

"Is that right? And what do you know that I don't know?" she asked, sticking her feet in her sandals.

"You're the one who always feels something. You tell me," she teased. "Come on, the stores are waiting."

They roamed the stores for hours. Zoe couldn't seem to find anything she liked and they had seen at least fifty dresses by Sharlene's last count.

"Girl, there has to be something that you like. Since when did you get so particular?" Sharlene pushed some dresses aside on the rack hoping to find something that would spark some interest. "How about this one?" She held up a spaghetti-strapped midnight-blue fitted dress that felt like silk to the touch and shimmered when it moved. "This is perfect. Slightly sexy and elegant at the same time."

Zoe looked at the dress then took it from Sharlene. She walked to a mirror and held it up in front of her. She turned right and then left to get the full effect. She spun toward Sharlene with a big smile on her face. "This is the one. It's perfect. I love it."

"Finally." Sharlene sighed. "Damn, this is the last time I'm going shopping with you for a big occasion."

"No, its not," she said with a grin.

"You're probably right."

They laughed and headed for the cashier.

* * *

"My mother said she was going to tell me about my father," Zoe blurted out while they walked back to Sharlene's car.

Sharlene slowed. "Say what?"

Zoe nodded. "We had a rather nasty conversation before I left for New York."

She went on to tell her how she'd blown up at her mother when she'd insinuated that it wasn't proper for her to be "staying" with a man that wasn't her husband. And what her response had been.

"Whoa. No wonder you've been so out of sorts. Between carrying that around, the situation with your job and keeping it all from Jackson... You're carrying around too many secrets, girl. You need to set some of those burdens down."

"I know. It's making me nuts." She pushed out a breath. "All my life I've wondered about my father. Was he dead or alive? Did I pass him in the street? Did he even know about me? You know what it says on my birth certificate for father?"

Sharlene shook her head no.

"It's blank. Do you have any idea what that feels like to look at that empty space?"

"I can only imagine, sis." She hooked her arm through Zoe's. "But the time seems to have come for a lot of changes in your life."

"It sure looks that way."

Chapter 25

Classes hadn't started yet but the professors had returned to campus for the prerequisite meetings and submission of lesson plans. Jackson was feeling good about the upcoming semester and was eager to get back in the saddle. That mess with the letter seemed to be a done deal, so that was one less thing he had to worry about. But what he was really looking forward to was heading back home to New Orleans and Zoe's birthday party.

She hadn't quite been herself since they'd returned from New York and he was hoping that being back with her family would lift her spirits. He'd been looking for the perfect gift and actually found it in New York. The real test of their relationship would come when he gave it to her.

"You sure it's cool for me to come to Zoe's party?" Levi asked him as they exited the building. "I mean it might just be a family thing."

"You're seeing my sister, right?"

"Yeah."

"Then that should answer your question." He slapped him on the back. "Of course it's cool. Zoe told me to make sure that you came. And I know Michelle wants you there."

Levi grinned. "I know it's only been a minute since we've known each other but that woman makes me happy."

"She's a good woman. And I'm not just saying that because she's my sister."

"I know. We're taking it slow. I don't want to be a rebound, know what I mean?"

"Yeah."

"She's filing for divorce."

"She told me." He glanced at Levi.

"It's still going to take her a while to get over things. But once that's done, then we can really decide how we're going to move forward."

"Like you said, take it slow."

"Yeah," he said thoughtfully.

"Did you make your reservations for the hotel?"

"Taking care of that today, for sure."

They crossed the grounds to the parking lot.

"So what did you get Zoe for her birthday?"

Jackson grinned. "Secret."

"From me?"

"Yeah, from you. I don't want it to slip out. And from what my sister says, we talk about everything," he said in a bad falsetto. "And Michelle can't keep a secret, period. I tell you, you tell her and she spills the beans to Zoe."

"Damn, man, it's like that. I thought I was your boy."

"You are and I want to keep it that way."

"That's cold. But just so you know, Michelle has been working on something that she plans to surprise *you* with."

"Oh, yeah. What?"

"I ain't telling." He chuckled and unlocked his car door. "See you later, man."

Jackson shook his head in amusement and walked toward his car. Just as he was about to get in he heard his name being called. He looked out across the rows of cars and saw a woman coming toward him. As she drew closer his stomach clenched.

"Professor Treme, can I speak with you a moment. Please?"

"Sure, Victoria, what is it?"

"I know the last time we spoke I left so much up in the air. I shouldn't have. I should have been up front and told you everything."

"I'm listening."

"Carla is my half sister."

"What? She never told me she had a half sister."

She lowered her head for a moment. "She wouldn't. I was the big family secret. Daddy's indiscretion. She was the one who put me up to it. She was paying for me to go to grad school, saying it was her way of making up to me for how I'd been treated by the family. She said she would keep paying under the condition that I send those letters to the school."

"Letters? There's more?"

She dug into her knapsack and pulled out about a dozen letters wrapped in a rubber band. "I told her I sent them, but after the first one, I couldn't do it." She handed them to him. "I found out what she did. All of it."

Jackson looked at the stack of letters then at Victoria. "Thank you. You gave up a lot. Why?"

"I can find a way to finish school. This isn't the way. I may be the family secret but my mother didn't raise me like that. I'm sorry, professor. I really am."

Jackson was speechless.

Victoria turned to leave.

"Wait."

She glanced over her shoulder.

"Come to my office next week. There's still some scholarship money available. I'll work it out, talk to the finance department. You can't give up on your education."

Her eyes lit up. "Really?"

"Yes. Really."

"Thank you, thank you so much."

"Next week. I have the same office hours."

"I'll be there."

Jackson mechanically got into his car. Carla. All this time it was her. He tossed the letters onto the passenger seat. The first chance he got he was going to burn them.

After dinner, Zoe and Jackson worked side by side in her kitchen putting away food and loading the dishwasher.

"I still can't get over that Carla would go to such lengths to get back at you."

"I never would have never imagined in a million years that she was capable of the things she's done." He put away the plastic container with the leftover jerk chicken.

Zoe leaned against the sink, wiping her hands on the dish towel. She angled her head to the side. "I'm proud of you for what you're going to do for Victoria."

"She didn't have to tell me anything. Worst, she could have gone along with Carla. I don't even want to think about what could have happened if she did."

Zoe squeezed his shoulder. "You did the right thing."

Jackson turned out the kitchen light and followed Zoe into the living room. This whole routine, this thing that they were doing seemed so easy and so right, he thought. They had a rhythm with each other. There were no rules and verbal expectations, they just instinctively knew what the other wanted

and needed. When he was with Zoe he was at peace
and all the rest of the world took a backseat. He
knew now more than ever that all of the signs, the
dreams and the decisions that led him to change the
course of his life were all the right ones. It led him
to Zoe.

She rested her head in his lap while the news
played in the background. This felt good, she
thought. For the first time in her life she'd let a
man get this close to her, get into her life on more
than just the surface. And it wasn't as scary anymore. If anything she wanted more of it. And that
was where things swerved so totally off course.
She couldn't have it both ways. She couldn't have
the career-changing job and the man of her dreams.
And that realization was slowly breaking her heart.

"You ready for your big day?" he asked softly.

She adjusted her position. "Pretty much."

"I'm really looking forward to meeting your
family. Especially your grandmother."

"I've been telling her about you, ya know." She
turned onto her back so that she could look at him.

"Good things, I hope, and not the parts about my
bad singing in the shower."

She laughed. "No, trust me, my lips are perma-
nently sealed on that one."

"Am I really that bad?" he asked looking
wounded.

She reached up and tenderly stroked his cheek.
"Yes."

Jackson tossed his head back and laughed. "I'll try to keep it to a low hum from here on out." His eyes moved over her face and the smile that was on hers, the light that was in her eyes, filled him. He loved her. From the bottom of his soul he loved this woman. She had yet to say she felt the same way. And even as a part of him believed that she felt the same way and just as strongly, there was the voice of doubt that still wouldn't let go.

"Levi, Michelle and Shay are going to drive down tomorrow evening. They're going to stay in the hotel."

"There's plenty of space at the house. I told Michelle she was welcome. Sharlene is staying and she's bringing Ray. They're going to drive down tomorrow."

"How big is this little house of yours?"

"From the road, it looks pretty standard, but the house runs all the way back to the end of the property line, stopping just before the lake. There are eight bedrooms and three full baths. And there are two guest houses on the property. They used to be slave quarters, from what my family told me. The same house that my great-great-grandmother was enslaved on."

"A lot of history there."

Yes there was, she thought. Yes, there was.

Chapter 26

The weather was typical August; hot and sticky and from the summers that they both remembered growing up in Louisiana, they hadn't seen anything yet.

They'd been on the road since sunup and the signs welcoming them to the state of Louisiana loomed ahead, with the exits for New Orleans to their right.

The closer they got to their destination the more anxious Zoe became. There were so many things she had to confront this weekend. She hoped she was up to handling it all. Not to mention that she had yet to tell Jackson that she was offered the job in New York and that she was taking it.

"Let me know where to turn off. I think I remember but I'm not sure."

She focused back on the road. "We still have a little ways to go." She peered in the side-view mirror and saw Sharlene's Volvo close behind. "About another twenty minutes." She leaned back and tried to slow the rapid beating of her heart.

Jackson steered the car along the winding path that was embraced on either side by towering maple and willow trees, partially obscuring the houses beyond. It was coming back to him now; his bike rides past "the white house" as the kids called it back then.

The road sloped slightly upward and then the house came into full view. It was much like he remembered it, he thought smiling wistfully. So this is where Zoe grew up, he thought as he drove along the gravel lane to the side of the house. And suddenly he felt connected to this place somehow in a way that he couldn't quite put his finger on. It was more of a sensation, as if he'd really been here before and not just passing by. But of course that was crazy.

"Well, this is it," Zoe said as they came to a stop.

Sharlene's car pulled up behind them.

Before they could get out of their cars, the door to Zoe's family home swung open and her mother and her two aunts came out to greet them with wide waves and big smiles of welcome.

The quartet trooped over to the front porch and they were immediately swept up in hugs and kisses even before introductions were made. Zoe instantly felt warm inside, surrounded by so much love. She missed this, she thought. She missed hearing her aunts fuss with each other about who burnt the corn bread or whose turn it was to weed the yard. She missed hearing her Nana's stories about growing up in this house and her daily advice about everyday living. She turned to her mother and realized that she missed her, too. And that surprised her more than anything.

"It's good to see you," her mother said softly, holding Zoe's arms in her hands.

"It's good to see you, too, Mama." She leaned in and hugged her mother and felt like a damn of tears was going to burst inside of her. She held on for a moment longer to pull herself together then stepped back. "Ya'll know Sharlene, of course," she said. winking at her friend. "And this is her friend Ray." She stepped next to Jackson. "This is Jackson Treme." She took his hand and held it tight. "Jackson, Ray…my aunt Flo, my aunt Fern and my mother, Miraya."

There was another round of hugs and cheek kissing now that the introductions were official.

"Ya'll come on in and get settled," Aunt Fern said. "We have lunch all fixed and Zora is waiting to meet ya'll."

"Let the children wash the dust off of 'em first, Fern," Flo fussed.

"Aw hush. You could at least offer them a glass of cold water, dusty or not."

"Don't you two start in front of company," Miraya warned.

Zoe waved her hand in dismissal. "Don't mind them," she said for Jackson and Ray's benefit, "that's their usual."

"Zoe, you want to show everyone where they're going to stay?" Aunt Fern asked. "The rooms are all fresh and there are towels in that hall closet. You remember the one."

"Yes, ma'am," she answered, suddenly feeling like a little girl again and not minding at all.

"Then ya'll come right back down," Miraya said.

"Yes, ma'am," came the chorused response.

Zoe led the guests through the house and up the stairs to the bedrooms and baths. "Sharl, you know your way around as well as I do."

"I'm going to take my same room. I used to stay here all the time when we were growing up," she said to Ray.

Zoe took Jackson's hand. "My room is this way." She turned left down the hallway and opened the door at the end.

The heavy four-poster bed dominated the space, but it was the sheer white curtains in the windows that softened the room. It was a simple room, and he could tell that it hadn't been used in a while. There were no personal effects around except for a framed photograph that sat on the nightstand. He walked over and picked it up. It was a picture of Zoe and her mother. The picture by her nightstand whether she still lived in this house or not spoke volumes about the way Zoe really felt about her mother. He gently put the picture back down.

He turned to her and found her watching him, expecting him to say something, it seemed. But they both knew that the one photograph in the room said it all.

"Is it really okay if we spend the night together in your room with your family right here?"

"I was planning on taking the room right next door," she said with a devilish smile. "So when you hear the secret knock, it's me."

"Hmm, nothing is more of a turn-on than sneaky sex," he teased, pulling her into his arms and nibbling on her neck.

Zoe squirmed and giggled. "Why, you bad boy," she said emphasizing her Southern belle charm. "I wouldn't know anything about that, sir, me being such a lady and all."

"Well, this bad boy would be more than happy to teach you everything he knows." He dipped his head for a kiss when the knocking on the door made them leap apart like two teenagers caught in the backseat.

Zoe tugged on her shirt and went to open the door.

"Ya'll coming or what?" Sharlene asked. "I'm starved and I want to see Nana."

"Yes, we were just coming down."

Sharlene looked from one to the other. "Hmm. Right."

"Come on, babe, before my *friend* tells on us." She stuck her tongue out at Sharlene and swept by her.

When they got downstairs they were drawn to the backyard by the sound of animated conversation and laughter.

The family was gathered on the enclosed porch with a spread of food that was fit for royalty. Nana sat regally at the head.

"It's about time," Aunt Flo fussed. "We were 'bout to eat all this without ya."

"Come on out here and set yourselves down," Aunt Fern ordered.

The long wood table was covered from end to end with food; from platters of golden fried chicken, catfish that had been dipped in Fern's special batter, deep dish macaroni and cheese, fresh cut string beans, seasoned collards and black-eyed peas and rice. And for dessert, peach cobbler and apple pie.

"Don't just stand there with your mouths open," Miraya gently chided, "get a plate and dig in."

Zoe took Jackson's hand and led him down to the end of the table where Nana sat, while the others started fixing their plates.

She bent down and kissed her Nana's cheek,

wrapped her arms around her neck, then knelt down beside her. "Nana Zora, this is Jackson Treme."

Jackson extended his hand. She took it in a surprisingly strong grip and eased him down to her. "We don't shake hands 'round here. We give hugs," she said in a voice that to Jackson sounded like a musical voice that he'd heard all of his life. He leaned down and hugged her and within the brief seconds of their embrace Jackson felt an enormous sense of tranquility wash over him, a feeling that no matter what happened, it was going to be all right.

When he stepped back her gaze connected with his and she smiled and said only to him, "Yes, it is."

Jackson blinked back his surprise just as Sharlene elbowed her way over to get in her Nana time.

"Come on let's eat," Zoe said. "I'm starved." She glanced up at him and registered the almost dazed look in his eyes. "You okay?"

He blinked and focused on her. "Yeah, fine. Your grandmother is special."

Zoe turned and looked behind her. Zora was being waited on hand and foot, her daughters tending to her every need without a word of direction or a request from her. "Yes, she is special."

"Hope you like everything," Zoe's mother said, coming up to stand beside her as she filled her plate.

"It's incredible. Really."

"We all worked hard to make it nice. And tomorrow will be even better."

Zoe smiled. "I can't imagine how."

Miraya patted Zoe's shoulder. "You'll see."

The late afternoon lunch turned into dinner complete with lively talk, plenty of laughter, gossip about the neighbors and anecdotes about the family as the food continued to flow.

As the sun began to set and the day grew cooler, Aunt Flo offered "something a little stronger to help you rest," she'd said.

To which Fern replied, "Don't you mean to help *you* rest?" And they were at it again.

Nana Zora interrupted the back and forth by announcing that she was retiring for the night. "Come help your grandmother to her bed," she said to Zoe.

"Good to have you back home," she said as Zoe helped her up the stairs.

"It feels good being here." She opened the door to Zora's bedroom.

"Come sit a minute," Zora said as she sat on the edge of her bed.

Zoe took a seat in the chair next to the bed.

"You have some decisions weighing heavy on you. And what you decide is gonna change your life. He's a good man. He's the one we've been waiting for, the one for you. Now I can't tell you what to do, but you'll know when the time comes."

"How will I know?"

"You're gonna feel the answer right here." She pointed to the center of her chest. "That's how you'll know. We Beaumont women have made some wrong choices throughout the years and not living up to what Zinzi had planned. And we done paid for it. You can make that right. Now go ahead. Tomorrow is your day and you need to be rested."

Zoe got up and kissed her grandmother's cheek. "Rest well."

"You do the same."

Zoe closed the door softly behind her. She had every intention of going to her room but her mother stopped her in the hallway.

"Your Nana, okay?"

"Yes, she's fine. Getting settled down."

"Good, good." She hesitated for a moment. "I wanted to give you your birthday present early."

"Mama, you don't have to do that."

"I want to. Come."

She followed her mother to the other side of the long winding hallway into her bedroom.

"Close the door."

Zoe did as she was asked while her mother went to her dresser and took out what looked like a photograph. She held it out toward Zoe.

"His name is Paul. Paul Randall. I met him when I was nineteen years old. He was something else," she said wistfully.

Zoe's hand began to shake.

"And he was going to do things with his life. Be somebody. He was in school to be a lawyer. So when I found myself pregnant, well, I couldn't tell him. I knew what he would do. He'd drop out of school, find some piece of job to take care of me and that baby and one day he'd wake up and hate me for taking his life away from him." She swallowed over the knot in her throat and vigorously shook her head. "I couldn't let him do that. Couldn't." She sniffed back her tears and lifted her chin. "So I went on, had my baby and had my life and gave him his."

Zoe could feel her heart beating wildly in her throat. "You...you never told him about me?"

Miraya shook her head, no. Her lips pinched into a tight line. "I thought that was love. Giving someone their freedom. Never giving them a chance to play their own version of what love was. Been looking for it ever since." She gave a sad smile. "In all those clubs and dives. Never found it again." She looked into her daughter's eyes. "I don't want that for you. When you have it, when you feel it, give it a chance. I didn't do right by you or by...your father. You can change all that. And maybe you can find it in your heart one day to forgive." A lone tear slid down her cheek.

Zoe wanted to be angry, furious at mother for what she had done. But she'd buried her anger long ago. She'd replaced it with dismissal and distance over the years to shield herself from hurt. But for the first time what she realized was that she hadn't lost out all those years. She'd been loved and doted on and cared about in every way possible. It was her mother who'd lost so much and now she wanted to ensure that Zoe didn't make her same mistakes. She gave her that part of her life back that had been missing. And now Zoe needed to return that gift with one of her own.

"I forgive you, Mama."

Zoe walked toward her mother as Miraya's arms opened wide and cocooned her in love.

Chapter 27

Zoe awoke the following morning to a cacophony of sound and activity. Cars, women's voices calling out directions, doors opening and closing. She pulled herself halfway up when her foot met with a solid object and she remembered that she and Jackson had spent the better part of the night talking and talking. He must have fallen asleep across the bottom of the bed.

Laughing she realized that this was the first night that they'd spent together and not made love. And it was all right.

"Hey, sleepy head," she softly called out, crawling to the bottom of the bed.

Jackson's eyes squinted open against the rays of

the morning sun. He looked around trying to get his thoughts to focus. "I must have fallen asleep," he said, his voice still thick and rough.

"You think!" she teased. "Come on and get up before someone sees you creeping out of my boudoir."

Before she could react Jackson had flipped her over and pinned her beneath him. "Happy birthday, baby."

She grinned. "Thanks." She pecked him on the lips.

"I would love for both of us to get in our birthday suits but sounds like the troops are up and active."

He rolled over and Zoe hopped off the bed. "Go, go before someone sees you," she said, shooing him out of the door. "What time will Levi and Michelle get here?"

"He said around noon. They were going to check in to the hotel first and then head over."

"Okay. I'm going to shower and get dressed. Sounds like they could use some supervision. I'll meet you out back when you're ready."

Zoe spun away from the door, feeling giddy inside. She was happy. Really happy and she was looking forward to whatever the day would bring her. She was finally ready.

When she came out back the massive lawn was covered with white circular tables and matching wooden chairs. A group of men from Nana Zora's church were struggling with putting up a tent and the ladies auxiliary were setting up the tables and spreading white tablecloths across them. The driveway was lined with cars filled with neighbors bringing trays of food, coolers and gift bags.

Zoe covered her mouth in shock. Her heart swelled in her chest. She couldn't believe that this was all for her. There were faces that she hadn't seen in years. All of them were there for her. Sharlene and Ray were already pitching in, wrapping up the trees with stringed balloons. Nana sat in her favorite backyard chair beneath the biggest tree at the far end of the yard, calling out directions like a drill sergeant between sips of what Zoe knew was mint julep.

"Happy birthday, baby," Aunt Flo said giving her a quick kiss as she ambled down the porch steps balancing a bowl of punch.

Aunt Fern was right behind her carrying a big metal wash bucket—for what, Zoe had no idea. "Happy birthday," she said on her way down the steps. "You best get out of the way or you'll get run down."

Another car tried to get onto the driveway but it was full. The driver parked and Levi, Michelle and Shay got out.

Zoe waved to them from the porch. They wound their way around the tables and people and finally reached her.

"Oh, my goodness!" Michelle exclaimed. "I had no idea. I was thinking a family gathering."

Zoe laughed with joy. "So did I. Hey, Shay, did you enjoy the drive?"

She bobbed her head transfixed by all of the activity.

"You find the place okay, Levi?"

"No problem. Where's Jackson?"

"Good question. He should be coming down soon. Can I get you all anything?"

"No, I'm good," Levi said. Michelle agreed.

"Okay, well, let me introduce you around."

By late afternoon the tables were set and decorated, the tent was up, the racks of food were being spread out on Sternos that stretched across four six-foot tables. Buckets of ice were still being brought in and the two grills were getting hot. The men from the church had set up a small stage for the blues band that Zoe's mother had hired and the yard looked like a fairy tale.

"Your family has gone all out," Jackson was saying as they stole a quiet moment alone.

"I can't believe this is all for me. I'm just without words."

Jackson hugged her. "You deserve it, baby."

"I better get dressed. And you, too. Nana said six sharp."

"Yes, ma'am."

Sharlene, Michelle and Zoe shared Zoe's bedroom mirror to finish their makeup and hair.

"I told you that dress was the one," Sharlene said as Zoe strutted across the room, did a pirouette then struck a pose.

"Jackson's eyes are going to pop," Michelle said.

"That's not all he's going to pop," Sharlene said with a snicker.

"Sharlene you are so awful," Zoe said, but she couldn't wait to get Jackson alone.

The music from the band floated up to the window.

"It's party time," Sharlene announced, wiggling her hips. "Let me go and find my man." She sashayed out and Michelle and Zoe followed suit.

"You know I've been working on the genealogical software program," Michelle was saying to Zoe while they walked down the hall to the stairs.

"Hmm, umm, how's that going?"

"Well," she said, in an excited whisper. "I decided to trace our family and I traced us all the way back to a small village in Mali."

Zoe face flamed. "What?"

"Yep. And the chief of the village had a son, Etu, who was captured and sold right here in New Orleans! He was our great-great-grandfather. Can you believe it?"

Zoe's temples began to pound. *Etu and Zinzi*. Oh, my God, Nana was right. She could barely breathe. "Did you bring the printout?"

"I think so. If I didn't leave it on the dresser. I

wanted to surprise Jackson, but at the last minute we started rushing…"

Zoe swallowed. "If you find it…I would love to see it."

"Sure."

They stepped outside and the party began.

Food and drinks flowed, laughter floated through the air on the notes of the band. Couples and singles danced across the grass. And as the sun began to set, the candles on each of the tables were lit.

"Happy, baby?" Jackson asked as they swayed to the music.

"Very."

The piercing screech of the microphone cut through the music followed by Miraya's voice.

"Can I have everyone's attention?" she shouted into the mike.

By degrees, the crowd quieted down.

"Thank you everyone for coming here today and for all the help in making this day special for my daughter, Zoe."

The crowd erupted into applause.

"I am thankful for my child. I wasn't always the mother that I should have been but I never stopped loving her. And because of the love she received from my mother, Zora, and my sisters, Fern and Flo, she is a wonderful, wonderful woman who makes me proud every day." She turned a bit toward the band and gave them a cue. Slowly she faced the audience and the swell of the Billie Holiday classic "God Bless the Child" moved easily like the Mississippi across the night.

"Them that's got shall get, them that's not shall lose…" Miraya's controlled contralto voice seeped into the souls of the listeners.

"…so the bible says but it still is news…"

Zoe felt tears sting her eyes. She hadn't heard her mother really sing in years and now she remembered the power of that voice and understood why she wanted to chase *her* life.

"…mama may have, papa may have…"

Jackson took her in his arms and they moved as one to the heartrending song.

"…but God bless the child that got his own that got his own…" The band held that last note of promise then faded out.

"Happy birthday, Zoe," Miraya said into the mike and the hundred plus guests erupted into the Happy Birthday anthem while an enormous cake was wheeled out on a cart, lit with what looked like a hundred candles instead of thirty.

Zoe was crying full-blown now, her eyes so cloudy with tears that Jackson had to lead her over to her cake.

"Make a wish!"

Zoe closed her eyes. She knew what she wanted. She knew it was possible—if she believed. She held Jackson's hand, took a deep breath and blew them all out.

Chapter 28

Levi, Michelle and Shay had returned to the hotel. The band was packed up and gone. The ladies from the church had packed up the leftover food to be given to the shelters and the homeless that visited the soup kitchen. The rental company would pick up the table and chairs in the morning. Nana and Zoe's aunts and mother had gone up to bed. Sharlene and Ray decided that the night was still young and drove into the Quarter. Jackson and Zoe sat together on the porch steps reveling in the magnificent day.

"What a day," Jackson said softly.

"Yes, it was." She leaned her head on his shoulder.

"Beautiful night for a beautiful woman."

Zoe sighed in utter contentment.

"Is that one of the guest houses you were talking about?" he asked, pointing to a small structure at the end of the property.

"Yeah, the former slave quarters. You want to see it?"

"Sure." He helped her to her feet.

"I haven't been in here in years," she said. "I have no idea what kind of shape it's in." She tugged on the door and it jerked open.

It was pitch dark inside. Zoe felt around for where she remembered the light to be and the room was bathed in soft light. Much to their surprise the room was in pristine condition. A double bed and dresser were the main pieces with two wing chairs against one wall. One narrow window looked out on the main house. There was a fireplace that had long been closed off.

Jackson walked around the small space feeling a connection that he couldn't explain. Although he knew he'd never been here before, if felt as if he had.

"There's something I need to talk to you about," Zoe said.

Jackson pulled back from the strange feelings and focused on Zoe. "Sure. What is it?"

Zoe sat down in one of the chairs. She patted the seat of the other. "There's so much," she began as he sat down. "I don't know where to start."

"Wherever you want."

"I know my father's name…" She told him about her mother's confession and the reason why she'd done what she did.

He took her hand. "How do you feel about what your mother did?" he asked gently.

She drew in a long breath. "I understand. It still hurts, but I understand. What it helped me to realize is that even when you love someone you can't make the decision on how they will love you back. That's why I'm telling you about the offer that the Guggenheim presented to me…"

Jackson listened, listened in between the words. When she'd finished she all but held her breath waiting to hear what Jackson had to say.

"I'm not going to make it easy for you," he said looking deep into her eyes. He dug in his inside jacket pocket and took out a small midnight blue velvet box, a perfect match to her dress.

Zoe gasped.

Jackson took her hand. "Marry me, Zoe. You are my past, my present and my future. I've spent my life becoming the man I am so that I can be the man you need. I don't care if you take a job in New York or the farthest reaches of the globe. We can do it together. Say yes, Zoe. Tell me you love me and say yes."

Her throat was so tight she could barely get the words out. "Yes, yes, I'll marry you. I'll marry you and love you for the rest of my life…just like I've always done."

He lifted the ring from its cushion and slowly slipped it onto her finger. It sparkled in the moonlight.

She reached for him while he reached for her and their mouths found each other in a kiss so sweet that it was that first kiss more than century ago, shared under the thatched roof beneath a summer's night sky, splashed with thousands of pinpoints of light. And the village rejoiced in their union.

And as Zoe gave herself willingly, with her heart and soul opened to Jackson, she fully understood her legacy. This was the reincarnation of the love of her ancestor Zinzi and his ancestor Etu. A love so strong that neither time nor death nor separation could stop their love. They would find it again.

Zoe would not make the choice of her mother, her grandmother and her aunts who had chosen not to give love a chance.

And the ancestors rejoiced at last.

Epilogue

Zoe and Jackson sat on the front porch of the Beaumont house. The summer breeze was filled with the scent of jasmine and a summer storm that hovered just beyond the horizon.

Zoe rocked Mikai on her lap and Jackson sung a lullaby to his twin sister, Mikayla. They were born nine months to the day of Zoe's thirtieth birthday. And on that night that they were conceived, the legacy was fulfilled and the curse of unfulfilled love was finally broken.

In the background, Zoe's mother was singing a Billie Holiday number and preparing to go out to dinner with that nice man Mr. Clarke that had been eyeing her for years. They'd been seeing each other for nearly six months now and her mother actually seemed happy.

Zoe had found her father. He lived in Nashville and she and Jackson were making plans to visit. She'd decided against the job in New York and as soon as her babies were old enough she planned to open a small art gallery in town. Jackson was teaching at the University and loved being back home again.

Aunt Fern and Aunt Flo were tending the garden, pulling weeds with Lucas Beniot and Randolph Porter, two men from the church that had been hanging around for a while now. Fern and Flo giggled like schoolgirls as Lucas and Randolph showed them the right way to pull weeds.

Nana lived long enough to see Zoe marry Jackson and hold her great-grandbabies. But she was never far. Her spirit was in all of them. And as soon as Makai and Mikalya were old enough, Zoe would tell them of their rich history and about the power of love that could overcome all obstacles. And she was certain that one day they would both find the love that she'd found with Jackson.

Jackson turned to his wife. "I love you."

"I know," she said. "I've always known."

* * * * *

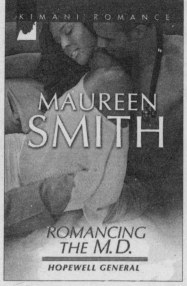

REQUEST YOUR FREE BOOKS!

2 FREE NOVELS
PLUS 2 FREE GIFTS!

KIMANI™
ROMANCE

Love's ultimate destination!